The Prestons Novellas

The Baron Without Blame

The Countess Without Conviction

Katherine Grant

This is a work of fiction. Names, characters, places, and incidents either are the product of the author's imagination or are used fictitiously. Any resemblance to actual persons, living or dead, events, or locales is entirely coincidental.

Print ISBN 979-8-9945595-0-5

Copyright © 2026 by Katie Flanagan

The Baron Without Blame copyright © 2021 by Katie Flanagan

The Countess Without Conviction copyright © 2024 by Katie Flanagan

No part of this publication may be reproduced in any form or by any means, including photocopying, recording, or other electronic or mechanical methods, without the prior written permission of the publisher or author, except as permitted by U.S. copyright law. This includes the use of any material contained herein for the purpose of training, integrating or incorporating artificial intelligence by any means or in any fashion. For permission requests, please contact the author here: katherine@katherinegrantromance.com

Cover design by Julia Gerbach

www.katherinegrantromance.com

Also by Katherine Grant

The Countess Chronicles:

The Ideal Countess
New Year's Masquerade
The Duchess Wager
The Husband Plot

The Prestons:

The Baron Without Blame

KATHERINE GRANT

The Viscount Without Virtue
The Governess Without Guilt
The Charmer Without a Cause
The Sailor Without a Sweetheart
The Countess Without Conviction
The Miss Without a Mister
The Widower Without a Will

Northfield Hall Novellas

(an unordered series for the mood reader)
The Hellion of Drury Lane
It's In Her Kiss
Three Nights With Her Husband
Letters to Her Love
In The Wide Open Light
Her Perfect Pirate

Plus, a free short story, The Spinster, available exclusively at www.katherinegrantromance.com

Dear Reader,

Enclosed in this paperback are two novellas that are each an important piece of The Prestons, my series about a radical Regency family trying to rewrite the rules of the world around them while falling in love.

In *The Baron Without Blame*, Lord Martin Preston and Lady Rosalind Turner agree to a fake engagement to keep up appearances, but as they share with each other their dreams for a better future, they begin to lose track of the lie.

In *The Countess Without Conviction*, Ellen Preston finds that moving into a new home nine years into her marriage tests her relationship with beloved husband Max in ways she never predicted, and together they must fight to find their way back to each other.

Up until now, these stories have been available exclusively as ebooks, mostly because they are too short to be cost effective for printing as single titles. By combining them into one edition, I can print them at a price that hopefully is not too exorbitant for readers.

This is exciting yet may cause some confusion about reading order. If you are new to the Prestons, then *The Baron Without Blame*, as the prequel novella, is the perfect place to start. However, I recommend holding off on reading *The Countess Without Conviction* until you have read at least *The Viscount Without Virtue*, if not all the titles that come before it.

If you are not new to the Prestons, then I invite you to read in whatever order you like. Let me know if you discover any hidden messages when reading backwards.

Thanks so much for joining me in this little corner of my imagination.

Happy reading!

Katherine

The Baron Without Blame

The Prestons Prequel Novella

Katherine Grant

WHAT TO EXPECT FROM THE BARON WITHOUT BLAME

Compromised over nothing, will this fake engagement lead to something?

> **This free prequel novella kicks off *The Prestons* series.**
> When Martin Preston, Baron Ashforth, is caught on a dark balcony with a debutante, **he does the right thing.** Even though he was only freeing her skirts from the railing. **Even though he doesn't know her name.** The next morning, he faithfully offers for her hand in marriage.

THE PRESTONS NOVELLAS

Lolly Turner has nothing against Lord Preston. He is handsome, kind, and honorable. Yet she can't bring herself to marry a man solely because of gossip. When she knows she should say yes, she says no. Instead, they concoct a false engagement: they tell the world they plan to marry, while in reality Lolly will jilt Martin once the scandal has died down.

Martin invites Lolly and her family to spend the Easter holiday at his country home to keep up appearances. As he and Lolly spend more time together, they share visions for the future and realize they both hope for a world very different from the one into which they were born. But when Lolly's father catches wind of their shared politics, he changes his mind about the wedding. **Which means it is up to Lolly and Martin to choose: should they do the right thing, or follow their hearts?**

For content advisories, please visit www.katherinegrantromance.com/contentadvisories.

CHAPTER ONE
LONDON, 1788

O N THAT MARBLE BALCONY of Lord Leighster's townhouse, wreathed by an overly-ornate iron railing, it occurred to Martin Preston that human sewage stank no matter in which city one found oneself. It fouled the sights of Calcutta as easily as it did Casablanca, sometimes stinking in town worse than seven weeks at sea. Even at this most magnificent ball in the great imperial center of London, Martin caught its unmistakable whiff above the fragrant springtime garden blooms.

It occurred to him, too, that the thought proved he was in no mood to fraternize at Lady Leighster's soiree. His head was too muddled from his travels, when instead he should be discussing the latest horse races or flirting with a pretty lady. He would do better to go straight home to his dark room and nurse a glass of Madeira. Except Madeira was out, since it arrived from the subjugated Portuguese colonies; and so too was his other old favorite, the smoking pipe, whose tobacco came from the slave trade. He would have to rely on warm milk, then, with a splash of honey.

Small comfort that would be.

Martin took another deep breath, trying to summon the proper spirits to return to the ballroom, when he realized that on top of the garden roses and the city stench, there was another scent. A better scent.

A human scent.

Then came the sneeze. It was louder than any sneeze had a right to be. Martin could practically hear the mucus propelling out the nose.

He wasn't sure which was worse: realizing he was not alone on the balcony or overhearing such a viscerally personal experience. He angled his shoulders away from the noise. Whoever was suffering such a violent eruption surely wanted their privacy. "I beg your pardon. I did not realize this balcony was occupied."

The sneezer sniffled methodically into a handkerchief. "The fault is mine. I did not make myself known."

The voice was female. Light, clear, and a faint flatness to her vowels that made Martin think of the far side of the ocean.

"I'm having an attack of allergies, I'm afraid. I blame Mr. Montague's cologne."

Martin swallowed back any reply. He should not be on a dark balcony alone with this voice.

"I thought you were my mother, which is why I didn't say anything," the voice continued before he could move. "She bid me wait here while she fetches more handkerchiefs from the retiring room. Only I've been waiting for eons. Perhaps she is having a nap."

An unchaperoned female voice. Now Martin really did reach for the door. "I shall fetch your mother for you. Whom may I inquire after?"

Her reply was another sneeze. Now that he knew his companion was female, he could revel in how unladylike the sound was. No wonder her chaperone had shunted her onto a dark balcony; no husband could be caught when one sneezed like a blacksmith.

"Bless you."

"Oh, I so hate allergies!" Her skirts rustled underneath this reply. Martin had an instant vision of Smyrna silk draped over the wide circumference of a pannier. Then – startlingly – he heard a soft thud, followed by a yelp.

Martin didn't dare turn around. "Are you quite alright?"

"Yes," the voice huffed. Then, reluctantly, "I suppose not. My skirts seem to have gotten caught on the railing."

Even in the darkness, Martin blushed. He most definitely should not be discussing skirts with an unchaperoned young lady.

He reined in his thoughts before they could race after images of petticoats and slim legs.

The most proper thing to do was fetch her chaperone. But if he left her alone on this balcony, someone else could just as easily step out and discover her trapped.

Which was how he found himself asking, "May I offer my assistance?"

There was a long, reluctant silence. Then, "I suppose so. Thank you."

Martin turned. He could just make out her silhouette, leaning awkwardly into the wall while her skirt ballooned against the wrought-iron railing. Her gown was pale – a virgin white, perhaps – and shone in the dim moonlight. The rest of her melted into the shadows.

Clearing his throat, he crossed to the railing. His guess was one of her pannier hoops had hooked onto an ornamentation. He knelt, all too aware of her perfume – which brought to mind a summer morning's mist – and tried to lift the skirt off the iron. He freed the hoop, but the silk overskirt still clung to the balcony, and Martin now saw it had been impaled, a long gash like a lightning bolt revealing the ruffled petticoat beneath.

He worked the silk carefully so as not to tear it any further. He had just freed it of the pineapple-shaped spear when the balcony doors swung open.

With a shriek, his companion jumped. She landed even closer to the wall. Most of her skirt went with her, but the triangle of fabric in Martin's fingers ripped away.

Which meant he had a fistful of her dress in his palm when he turned to face the new arrival.

O F ALL THE PEOPLE who could have thrown open the balcony doors at that exact moment, it had to be Phoebe Leighster. Phoebe, who considered herself so clever to have married a marquess last year. Phoebe, who made up for her lack of friends by gossiping about anyone and everyone. Phoebe, who dramatically screamed, "Not Lolly Turner!"

Lolly straightened squarely onto her two feet and pressed both palms onto her pannier, as if that would sort everything out. "Lady Leighster, how clever. Have you seen my mother?"

This did not sort everything out. No sooner had Lolly gotten the word "mother" out than did Mama arrive, stopping short just behind Phoebe, her rouged lips opening into a horrified "o."

"My skirts got caught on the balcony." Lolly addressed this to Mama. "This gentleman was kind enough to free them for me."

The gentleman in question was still crouching. As if cued by her words, he stood, and Lolly stole a look at him. Before, she had only been able to make out a general shape. He was tall, that much she had gathered; now she took in the fashionable wig; a slim nose; silver and blue silk stretched across broad shoulders; strong legs in breeches and stockings.

A dashing figure to match his deep, velvety voice.

She looked away. His handsomeness would only hurt the situation, so there was no point in delighting in it.

"Lord Preston, I am shocked!" Phoebe Leighster declared. She did look rather horrified, and Lolly wondered if she had extramarital designs on this Lord Preston.

He was a baron, if Lolly remembered the family correctly, and only recently inherited. She stole another glance; yes, now she saw the black crepe ribbon tied about his left arm. The poor man was still in mourning, and now caught on a balcony with her.

"You have not been introduced," Mama said, her dark eyes turning from Lolly to Lord Preston and back again.

"No, I'm afraid not," Lord Preston said. "I did not realize the balcony was occupied until Miss Turner sneezed, and then I hesitated to leave when she was indisposed by...a mischievous wardrobe."

Lolly knew he hesitated because it was indecent to mention her skirts, but she also heard how it sounded. To her mother or to Phoebe – or to her father, who unfortunately Lolly now spotted fast approaching – it sounded like Lord Preston was searching for some explanation to cover a clandestine kiss.

She wished it had been a clandestine kiss. At least that would have been worth all this fuss.

Lolly held up the offending skirt as proof. "You see? My dress is quite ruined. We must go home at once."

Except here came her father. He hovered behind Phoebe Leighster for all of two seconds. Then, with frighteningly white lips, he stepped onto the balcony. "What is going on here?"

"It was my allergies," Lolly tried to explain. Mama spoke at the same time: "I only left her alone for a moment!"

But it was Phoebe Leighster who spoke loudest. "Lolly Turner, caught on the balcony with a man she hasn't been introduced to!"

Lolly felt a hundred eyeballs turn towards the balcony. She wondered what the other guests could see from the ballroom. The white silk in Lord Preston's hand? The red of her nose from such terrible sneezing? Or just the horrified backs of her parents and Lady Leighster?

Her father looked her over once more. Then he turned. "Well, Preston?"

Panic surged into Lolly's throat. She needed to stop this. She needed to explain. But when she opened her mouth, the air – filled with perfumes and colognes and flowers and city fumes – tickled her throat and nose, and she couldn't help it.

She sneezed again.

And Lord Preston had no choice but to say, "I shall call upon you tomorrow, Lord Turner, to make a formal offer."

Chapter Two

London townhouses all looked the same to Martin. Too slim, too tall, with windows staring blankly into the gray streets. The Turner residence was no different, even with potted flowers blooming at either corner of its door. The liveried butler accepted Martin's card on a shining silver tray, then escorted him directly to Turner's study without seeing if anyone was at home.

Martin supposed they had been waiting all morning for him to call.

What a sticky situation.

He would have married in the next few years, anyway. After all, he had the title now, and the land, and everything that went with it. Just last night, his peers had been all too eager to tell him what to do with it. The most obvious of which was to find a wife and see to heirs.

It was only that Martin hadn't yet aligned himself to that goal. He didn't know what kind of wife he wanted, whether he needed someone who could support a political career or someone who wanted seven children or someone who would simply leave him be.

He had hoped to solidify his other plans before asking a poor soul to trudge alongside him.

Turner awaited him behind a giant desk made of imported mahogany. Martin wondered if it came from the Spanish colonies or the British West Indies. Turner himself was in a dark coat over pale green cotton breeches. They both wore white wigs; this was a formal visit, after all.

"Lord Preston." Turner gestured to a red leather chair.

A perverse part of Martin – the little boy in him who screamed I did nothing wrong! – wanted to refuse it. Instead, he sat.

"You find my daughter irresistible," Turner said. Martin hated to note the hint of kindness in his eyes. "I do not blame you. However, I must hold you accountable to it."

Last night, after the disaster at the Leighster ball, Martin had raked through his copies of Debrett's and Burke's to find the Turner family. They had been knighted under Charles II and awarded an earlship by William and Mary. The Turner facing Martin now was the second son of the second earl; when his brother died prematurely eight years ago, he had inherited. Burke's listed three daughters, all of marriageable age, none of whom were named Lolly.

It was a common enough nickname. Martin only wished he knew whether he was betrothed to Rosalind, Charlotte, or Louisa.

"I apologize for causing a scene last night." That was as far as he would go in an apology. He could not find it in himself to apologize for whatever gossips of the ton seemed to think he had been doing, nor could he apologize for choosing to help Lolly when she was in distress. "I, of course, should like to offer to marry her."

Turner smiled. "Tell me about what settlement you can offer her."

Martin obliged, outlining his annual income, his property holdings, and the pin money he was prepared to guarantee his wife. He was not the richest bachelor in London, but neither was he the poorest, and considering everyone seemed to think he had compromised Lolly last night, Turner didn't have much choice in accepting. Still, the old man negotiated an extra three hundred pounds per year for her pin money.

"She will want for nothing," Martin said, though he feared it was a lie.

She might want for some things. For example, a husband interested in the normal pursuits. A husband who relished in importing goods from exploited lands. A husband more concerned with chasing thousands of pounds than doing the right thing.

Turner shook his hand. "The ladies await us upstairs. Let us go make their mornings joyous."

The upstairs drawing room was surely the most fashionable room in the house. The walls were draped in a pale pink damask pattern, and the furniture was all gleaming wood with silk-covered cushions. An expensive oil painting of the French countryside hung above the marble mantle.

As the centerpieces of the room were the Turner women. There were four of them, all bent over embroidery as if they hadn't the faintest idea something momentous was occurring. Martin surveyed them: the mother with silver hair, a blonde in green, a brunette in blue, and another brunette in yellow.

Martin's stomach sank. On the balcony last night, Lolly had worn a wig, not her natural hair. The sisters were close in age, the eldest twenty-three and the youngest nineteen, so he couldn't use that as a deductive device, either. He could only hope Turner didn't expect him to greet the correct girl without any introduction, or else he might never live down the embarrassment.

"Rosalind." Turner clasped his hands behind his back. "Lord Preston would like a moment alone with you."

The eldest sister, then. At least he knew her name now. As if the moment were slowed to the pace of sludge, Martin watched the ladies react. Lady Turner lifted her head directly, a twinkle in her eyes as she regarded him. The blonde and the brunette in blue elbowed each other. And the brunette in yellow – she was the one who stood.

Martin's heart skipped a beat. Of excitement, he supposed. Or perhaps relief. Or perhaps simply acknowledgment: this was happening. He was marrying this woman with fierce allergies and misbehaving skirts and false names.

This was his Lolly, whether he liked it or not.

Turner led them to a smaller sitting room, then retreated, closing the doors with a wink.

Martin felt a sudden wave of embarrassment. It was one thing to accept Turner's insinuations on his own. It was another to do so with Lolly at his side. It felt almost as if they were conspiring. Only he couldn't think what they were conspiring to do.

Lolly stood as far away from him as she could within the confines of the room. Her face was turned not towards him but to the window. She was of an average height, her hair the light brown of a dusty road, her skin more olive than cream. He noted what he could not see the prior night: thick eyebrows knitted in doubt, a brown mole dotting the crest of pink lips, rounded shoulders, distracting breasts rising from the pressure of her corset.

Martin hadn't expected such a beautiful wife.

He cleared his throat. "Lady Rosalind, I have come to offer my hand in marriage. Would you do me the honor of being Baroness Ashforth?"

The words were new to him, but they sounded right, hanging in the air. It was a strange start, to be sure, but it was what fate had decided for him. Martin couldn't bring himself to resent it.

Except Lolly regarded him with one, swift look that swept from his head to his toes. Then, returning her attention to the window, she said, "No."

THE NIGHT HAD NOT been kind to Lolly. First with the allergies, then with the scandal, and finally, with not sleeping for even an instant. Her neck ached from trying so hard to find comfort on the pillow. It did not help that now her whole body trembled, even her stomach.

She could feel Lord Preston's eyes boring into her. She imagined they were filled with shock. Perhaps injury, too, which would morph into anger soon enough.

Lolly had not planned to refuse him. When she opened her mouth, she expected it to say "yes." It was the only sensible reply.

And yet. She had said no. It had welled up from somewhere deep inside her, hot and red and demanding. It had nothing to do with Lord Preston and everything to do with the way Papa hadn't even cared whether a kiss had actually happened or not.

Lord Preston cleared his throat, a staccato cough that resounded through the room. "May I ask why you refuse? I am sure you know that we were compromised last night."

Compromised. Lolly wanted to laugh. If only he had compromised her. That would be worth all this excitement. Instead, they were in this mess over a little dash of petticoat. "Yes, you must regret ever offering to help me."

Lord Preston did not immediately respond. Lolly heard him move further into the room. She braced her hand on the windowsill.

"I do not regret it." His voice was so deep and soft. It wrapped about her like a velvet cloak. "I am a gentleman, Lady Rosalind. I could not in good conscience leave you alone on that balcony, when someone with worse motives than I could easily find you. It is perhaps unfortunate that the rest of Society is jumping to conclusions, but I do not mind accepting the consequences."

The consequences being her. Lolly knew he was trying to be kind. And she did not particularly care for romance. But she hated that this, her first proper proposal, was only predicated upon her being a yoke around Lord Preston's neck.

"Perhaps you would like to know more about me," he continued. "My seat is in Berkshire. It is not grand, but it has ample land and a comfortable home. I have one younger brother, who resides in Calcutta. I have recently returned from traveling in India and Africa. As my wife, you would have a generous allowance, and I imagine we could sort out living arrangements to suit your tastes."

He didn't so much stop speaking as much as he trailed off, as if realizing his words didn't sum into an argument. Or perhaps realizing his argument wasn't working.

"Lady Rosalind, while we do not know each other, circumstances have thrown us together. One might presume destiny – or an omniscient hand – has seen fit that we should be together. I promise to be a kind and dutiful husband. Mightn't you reconsider and make me an honorable man?"

"You are already kind and dutiful." Lolly turned to face him. It was the least she could do, though she regretted it almost immediately. He was so perfectly handsome, even with his hands clasping the back of a chair and his eyebrows knit in frustration. Her heart stammered a little at the sight. "It is not you, my lord, that I protest.

It is the situation. You may believe in this omniscient hand. I believe in my principles. I have done nothing wrong, therefore I see no reason to react. One must make decisions for good reasons, and the fact that Phoebe Leighster is making a fuss seems to me the worst reason in history."

Again, Lord Preston was silent for a long moment before responding. He drew his hands behind his back as he contemplated her. Lolly resisted the urge to turn back to the window. She had no reason to hide from him. The most any person could ask from another was honesty, and that was what she offered him now.

Finally, Lord Preston spoke. "I must admire your conviction. Too few people in our set live by principles alone."

"Thank you." Her fingers, clasped carefully behind her back, began to tremble. She hadn't been sure what to expect from his reaction. She didn't know what to do with acceptance.

"It is for the best, I suppose," he continued. "I will not make a typical husband."

Lolly opened her mouth to ask what he meant, when he had just promised to be kind and dutiful. She closed it. The question was bait, surely, and she would not be the fish who nipped at his hook.

And then – of course – a dust mite caught in her nose. She was so surprised by the sneeze that it was all she could do to catch it in her hand.

Lolly turned back to the window, mortified, trying desperately to think of what to do with the slime of snot that had dislodged into her palm.

"Bless you," Lord Preston said. "I hope you are in good health."

"It is only allergies. I am plagued by them in the city." Sometimes in the country, too, but Lolly didn't feel she needed to embarrass herself any further by making Lord Preston think her a constant mucus drip.

"Yes, the air here has its own peculiar properties."

Pulling her handkerchief from the depths of her skirt pocket, Lolly wiped her palm as surreptitiously as she could, then her nose, before turning back to face him. For some reason, he was smiling. Lord Preston's smile was the least perfect thing about him: it thinned his lips and slanted them to the left, in addition to revealing a set of crooked teeth. And yet, his whole countenance was so much more handsome with it on his face.

He sobered once more. "Lady Rosalind, what does your family think of your resolution against marrying me?"

Lolly ran the handkerchief beneath her nose again, if only to find more time to answer the question. Lord Preston thought her refusal premeditated. She supposed there was more honor in putting hours of thought behind it, and so she didn't admit that she was guided only by instinct. "I haven't spoken to them about it. I did try to tell my father the truth about what happened last night, but he doesn't seem to believe me."

She wasn't sure if Papa didn't believe her or didn't care about the truth; either way, she had tried to tell him the whole story all morning, and he only held up a hand and decreed it didn't matter.

Her decision would change things. Refusing Lord Preston amid scandal was as good as declaring herself unmarriageable. Lolly would have to come up with a plan, one that would shield her family from damage as much as possible.

And even then, Papa might never speak to her again.

"No, the facts don't have much import to the larger world. Which is why I would propose an alternate plan. One which will satisfy all parties: gossips will see a happy ending, your family will be saved from disgrace, and you will not end up married to me."

Lolly couldn't imagine what he had in mind.

"Accept my offer. I will invite your family to spend the Easter holiday at my home at Northfield Hall with the understanding that you and I are getting to know each other before planning an autumn wedding. The ton will be satisfied we are serious and move on to the next salacious gossip. Then, you may jilt me in the quiet of summer, by which point there will hardly be any scandal at all."

It was a ridiculous concept. Lolly could not lie. Not to the ton, and certainly not her family. And yet, was it more ridiculous than signing her whole life away simply because a kind man helped free her skirts from a bit of iron?

She eyed Lord Preston. He was so magnificently perfect, from the carve of his face to the way his feet shifted uncertainly to await her answer. He was certainly the most handsome man who had ever paid her attention; that he was doing so only because he had the bad luck to happen upon her sneezing couldn't lessen that fact.

Yet handsomeness was perhaps an even worse reason to marry. Or pretend to marry.

Lolly wasn't at all sure she could pretend.

Just then, the door opened, and Papa stepped into the room. He wore a ridiculous grin. "Well, may I offer my congratulations?"

Lord Preston looked to her. He raised one eyebrow, an expression that would have been cocksure on any other man. On him, it was simply kind.

"Yes," Lolly said. With one word, she answered her father's question, accepted Lord Preston, and condemned herself to a hell of falsehoods.

But Lord Preston smiled again, and she couldn't quite bring herself to regret it. Yet.

Chapter Three

It had been nearly five years since Martin had last seen Northfield Hall. Nearly five years since he had munched on Cook's famous oatcakes and skipped over the creaky step on the back stairs and ran his hands across the wild grass sprouting beside the pond. He wondered if it would be smaller than he remembered. If the fields would be more fallow than the rich, always-abundant ones in his memory. If, like London, Northfield Hall would look gray and decrepit and carry the faint scent of urine.

They had been travelling a day and a half, delayed at Reading by a rainstorm, and now in a matter of hours, Martin would be home. He hadn't expected to return so soon. His plan had been to stay in London through the close of Parliament and only then take his father's place at Northfield.

But it had seemed the sensible option to make it appear that he and Lolly intended to marry without the eyes of the ton dragging on their every move. Martin still couldn't quite believe she had agreed to the scheme – not after she had been so adamant to refuse him. But

Lord Turner had taken her "yes" and quite happily moved forward. The engagement was printed in the morning newspaper. Their trip to Northfield Hall formalized. Martin rented a horse, wrote ahead to his staff, and gave his London servants the week off.

And now they were passing through Thatcham, only five miles from Northfield. Martin knew High Street the way he knew his own heartbeat. The black-beamed Tudor buildings mixed with white cob shops. The gleaming stone church with its belltower rising towards the clouds. Dirk the blacksmith, glaring at his fire. Mrs. Chusley, always sitting on the steps of her family's rope shop, knitting away as she waited for customers. And, as they turned off the highway onto Northfield Lane, the green commons dotted with sheep and cows and pigs that ran all the way up to the hall.

Returning to London had plunged Martin into despair, because in the end, it wasn't better than any of the other cities he had visited around the world.

Returning to Thatcham was a completely different experience. His heart suddenly felt so light that he might have floated out of his body, watching himself canter down the lane with a smile from ear to ear.

The road veered northward, into a field of barley, and the old chalk hills filled the horizon. A white, centuries-old horse was carved into the hillside, stealing the view. It was huge, large enough to be seen for miles, its head lying to the east and its tail tapering in the grass to the west. Martin had taken it for granted all his life; now he marveled at it. How big it was. How ancient. How mysterious, that a civilization no one remembered would take the time to carve a picture into a hill.

He twisted in his saddle to see if the Turners were reacting as much as he. A train of carriages followed him: one large and fine conveyance carrying the Turner family and two smaller ones trailing with their staff and luggage. Even Lord Turner rode inside rather than on a horse because of a bad back. Martin couldn't see a single face, only the emblazoned family seal.

He settled back, trying not to let disappointment affect his mood. Even if they were getting married, Martin didn't need Lolly to stand in awe of his home. As it was, she would never be his wife, and therefore, he had no reason to seek her opinion on anything.

Martin hadn't proposed the trip to Northfield Hall with any hope of swaying Lolly. She had refused him with such certainty, that when the idea popped into Martin's head, he had only thought of saving them both from tongue wagging in the gossip sheets. But the image of her framed in the window, arguing about the principle of the thing, remained with him. And it had crossed his mind, once or twice, that perhaps he could change her mind in this one week.

They had spent limited time with each other on the journey so far. He had seen her only at meals, and then he always ended up seated beside Lady Turner. Martin couldn't explain why his eyes snapped to Lolly or why his ears strained to catch her words. He only knew that they did. And that his thoughts kept drifting to her – at first, to how she could have formed such a character as to refuse marriage on principle. Now, they brought her into almost any thought: what was

Lolly's opinion of horses? What did she make of the characters they encountered at the traveling inns? Did she always look so becoming in blue, or was that a function of firelight? How soft was her skin? Did she sneeze when kissing? Had she ever been kissed?

More and more, Martin had to restrain his thoughts from wandering down inappropriate paths.

He recentered his attention on that chalk hill in the distance and the solid horse beneath him. Only a few more miles and he would be home. Only a few more months, and he wouldn't have reason to think of Rosalind Turner at all.

And then, before he knew it, Northfield Hall appeared before him. Smoke rose from all seven chimneys, evidence that his staff had received his preparatory letter. The house itself was a hodgepodge of styles: only the east wing survived from the original Tudor architecture, the rest of the building unfurling in red brick and slate roof. A modest circular drive of packed dirt led to the front steps, which were Italian marble imported by Martin's grandfather. As Martin approached, old Fred Pryor appeared from the stable to catch the horses.

It was almost as if Martin had never left. Except Fred boasted even less hair than ever, and instead of Mrs. Jenkins – who had retired two years ago – a new housekeeper ordered the staff into a reception line. And, of course, except for the glaring absence of his father, brother, and even mother, who had already been gone ten years.

The closest thing to family was Mr. Maulvi, the Ashforth private secretary, emerging from the house in the customary gray waistcoat that set off his brown skin and the barest twinkle of a smile on his lips. It was so startling to see the man in flesh again after corresponding with him for five years – this man, who Martin had known since birth, who had quietly managed the estate for decades – that Martin very nearly bounded up the steps to clasp him in a hug. He locked his hands together, instead, and turned his attention to the guests.

The Turner ladies were spilling out of the carriage. They wore matching traveling costumes: Lady Turner in a deep maroon and the three sisters in forest green. Although the color richened Lolly's hair, her skin was pale from motion sickness, and almost as soon as she stepped foot on the solid ground, she sneezed.

Martin bit back a smile. Her sneezes were so ridiculous, so unladylike, that he couldn't help being charmed by them.

Her family didn't have the same reaction. Lord and Lady Turner both glared at her, while the blond sister rolled her eyes and the brunette giggled. Blushing, Lolly blew her nose into a wrinkled handkerchief. Her eyes swung up, landing on him.

That invisible touch was too intense. As if she could see straight into his mind. Or under his clothes. Martin looked away, spreading his grin to welcome Lord and Lady Turner to Northfield Hall.

They followed the script of a fashionable family arriving at a country home. The servants curtseyed, then disappeared. Martin led the Turners on a tour of the house, explaining the fire of 1682, the mythical creatures carved into the banisters, and apologizing for the outdated Rococo style that followed them from room to room.

"Not to worry, my lord," Lady Turner tutted, sliding a proud smile towards Lolly. "That is what a wife is for."

Lolly looked sick again, and Martin's confidence slithered down a notch.

He ended the tour in the back sitting room. It had been his mother's favorite room, updated every year with something new, and now it was a confectioner's blend of yellow silk wallpaper, red chinoiserie tables, pastel chairs, and a gleaming white mantlepiece. It boasted two walls of windows, catching the light almost all day, and now a beam of sunshine filled the whole room.

Mrs. Smollett arranged a tray of cold meats and a pitcher of lemonade on the table, then withdrew so that only a footman remained among them. Drawing her great skirts about her, Lady Turner landed on the pink sofa, triggering everyone else to sit, too. "Rosalind," she commanded, "pour the lemonade."

Lolly obeyed, silently. Meanwhile, Lord Turner picked up the conversation. "A fine home, as you said. Could use a little updating, but of course, you have only just inherited the title. With a little investment, you could make this one of the finest houses in England."

Lolly handed Martin a glass of lemonade. For the briefest of seconds, her fingertips brushed against his. Her eyes, surprised, darted up. Martin looked away before he could see any more of her reaction.

"You could receive the King as it is right now, of course," Lord Turner was saying, "but I've a design in mind that would only take three or five years, and then it would be fit for His Majesty."

Martin couldn't guess why he would care about preparing his house for a royal visit, when everyone knew King George never traveled farther from London than Weymouth. "Indeed?"

"Oh yes. I've quite a few ideas already. Shall we go for a tour of the grounds tomorrow morning, then?"

Having never been engaged to marry before – in fact, never even having close friends go through the process – Martin supposed this was normal behavior for a father-in-law. Advice was the purview of families, and Lord Turner was about to be Martin's family. In theory.

In practice, it felt rather like a hundred-pound stone had been tied about Martin's neck, laced with a steel chain of deceit.

There was likely a cleverer response. At the moment, Martin could only summon acquiescence. "Tomorrow morning, then."

Satisfied, Lord Turner bit into a ration of ham. The room was silent, save for a nervous titter from Charlotte. Martin watched as Lady Turner raised two imperial eyebrows at Lolly.

As if a puppet, Lolly opened her mouth. "We have been reading the newspapers on our journey. I wonder, Lord Preston, how you form an opinion of Mr. Hastings, since you have recently traveled to the East?"

Martin had been reading the papers, too, not only over the past few days but over the past few months, first in India and now here. Warren Hastings, former Governor General of Bengal, was charged with corruption.

He shifted his cup from one hand to the other, weighing his answer. Martin had a very strong personal opinion: Hastings was only a scapegoat for the very real problem of Englishmen making their fortunes on the backs of trusting Indian kingdoms. But it was popular among men like Turner to skewer Hastings, as if impeaching the one man would rid the Empire of its sickness.

Martin had never yet been able to win an argument against that kind of bombastic rhetoric.

"I have not met him in person," Martin said carefully, "but I have met many men like him."

Lord Turner shook his head. "The common man is not equal to the task of governing. That is the issue at heart, not the errors of one governor. I was saying this to the prime minister not three days ago, but of course, he wouldn't listen."

This was the other argument Martin tired of hearing. The East India Company had installed itself in the governments of India in order to better control trade, and now the peers in the House of Lords chose to blame all woes on the fact that merchants lived as kings.

He opened his mouth to parry, but Lolly beat him to it. "Was not John Adams the simple son of a farmer in Braintree, and now he is the ambassador to our King?"

She said this with a practiced nonchalance. Martin watched as Lord Turner first drew his brows together in annoyance, and then – receiving a game, playful smile from Lolly – softened into a doting father. "Would that I could view the world through the eyes of a woman or a babe, eh Preston?"

Before he could think, Martin forced a chuckle. It was the wrong thing, of course. He knew it immediately. But he was so much more comfortable humoring rather than arguing. He didn't even regret it until Lolly stiffened. In the same instant that Lord Turner changed the subject, pleased with himself, Lolly disappeared back into the pale, listless stick she had been this past day and a half.

Martin looked away. Up at the ceiling. Down at his plate. Anywhere but at Lolly. No wonder she refused to marry him. Even now, in the safety of his own home, Martin couldn't help her. Couldn't protect her from set-downs and rumors and barbs. He was nothing but an idealist without backbone, a dreamer without reality.

She poured him more lemonade, and he accepted. There was nothing else to do.

LYING DID NOT GROW easier. Lolly had hoped that the more she promised to marry Lord Preston, the less her stomach would clench in protest. Instead, by their first morning in Northfield Hall, she felt permanently queasy.

Lolly had only ever visited relatives at their country homes. She was accustomed to running off with cousins to explore the grounds or participating in organized parlor games. Northfield Hall felt empty in contrast, no one around but the servants passing from room to room. Papa and Lord Preston went off touring the property before Lolly arrived to breakfast, and she spent the morning sewing with Mama, Charlotte, and Louisa. She tried to concentrate – she was adorning a pair of stockings as a gift for Papa – but where usually embroidery calmed her mind, that day it only scattered it further. Each push of the needle reminded her she had put herself in this situation; each pull told her she would soon meet her punishment.

It didn't help that Charlotte and Louise wouldn't stop talking about her marriage. "It's not so fine a house that you can brag about it to Ursula," Louisa – the most pragmatic of her sisters – reasoned, "but it is a fine house, and with the improvements Papa suggests you may be proud of it."

"Pride goeth before the fall," Mama scolded. "Lolly will be happy in whatever house her husband provides her."

"I think it is romantic," Charlotte sighed. "He's so madly in love with you he wanted to bring you home immediately."

Lolly turned her head so Mama wouldn't see her roll her eyes. As if love had anything to do with this whole ridiculous scheme.

"Why must you wait until autumn to marry?" Louisa asked. "It's not as if you need delay for him to inherit his title or get back from a Grand Tour."

Mama cleared her throat in the way she did when she disliked a subject. "Your stitches are growing sloppy, Louisa."

Lolly luxuriated in silence for all of a minute before Charlotte looked dreamily out the window. "How wonderful, to love a man so much as to meet him on a dark balcony at a ball. There Louisa and I were, having an absolutely boring time talking to Lord Leighster, and you had an assignation!"

This, at least, she had never lied about and never would. "For heaven's sake, Charlotte, are you twenty-one or twelve? You know very well I had never even met Lord Preston and it was all a giant, unfortunate misunderstanding!"

Mama's sharp dark eyes settled on her. Lolly bent over her embroidery hoop, wishing she could take back the outburst. She knew the rebuke that was coming: she mustn't say such things, she must be grateful, she must forget she ever had any feelings other than love for the great Lord Preston.

Only it wasn't Mama who spoke next. It was the lord himself, in a voice just as deep and silky and smooth as that night on the balcony. "Forgive me for interrupting. I wondered if Lady Rosalind might accompany me on a walk?"

Lolly shot a glare at Charlotte, who was tittering nervously, then rose, setting her embroidery in its basket. "Thank you, my lord. I would enjoy that."

They went out a back door, directly into the tidy garden. It was an uncertain day, the sun shining one moment and the next hiding behind wet clouds, and the spring flowers looked a little tired from being cheerful for so long. Like the rest of the house, the garden was neither large nor impressive. Most of it served the kitchen, with a few ornamental plantings towards the back. If she were his wife, she would plant a rose garden and lilac tree and a hedge maze.

Lolly yanked her thoughts away from that train of thought. She would not be his wife, and she had better not start believing her own lies.

"Did you have a pleasant morning?" she asked, since Lord Preston had not started any conversation yet. "You must be glad to be home."

He looked over his shoulder, then drew her through the garden gate into the park beyond. "I confess I asked you on a walk for a respite. While it is good to be home, Lord Turner has many ideas for how a son-in-law should conduct business."

That did sound like Papa. He didn't stand for idleness, nor did he believe in keeping his opinions to himself.

"I am not used to this level of deceit," Lord Preston added. "At least between the two of us, there is no need for falsehoods."

"I am as exhausted as you, my lord. My sisters speak of nothing but our marriage."

"Good, then let's not even mention it when we are alone." He led her onto a green path that cut between two fields. The prospect was clear with brown, recently sown fields stretching like patchwork across a gently rolling landscape. On the horizon were larger hills, the huge white horse centering them like a cloud fixated in the sky. Lolly supposed the place was so beautiful she could walk for hours without realizing it.

Lord Preston gestured ahead of them. "Your father would have me enclose these fields from the people of Thatcham, so as to earn a profit."

His tone was carefully neutral, which snagged Lolly's attention. "You don't agree?"

"I'm not sure of my opinion. I am not as confident in my principles as you." Lord Preston swatted away a small buzzing insect that had started following them.

First, he claimed he would make a poor husband, and now he disparaged his own character. Lolly couldn't let the subject simply disappear into the chilled air. "Wise men seek counsel before making decisions. I won't hold it against you if you change your mind."

They took a few more strides down the path with only the sound of the breeze between them. Then Lord Preston said, "I spent the last five years touring the Empire. I wanted to understand our commerce. The pepper farms, the cotton factors, the tea warehouses. I am not sure what I expected, but I suppose I thought the people we met would fall to their feet in gratitude. After all, we must have brought them great wealth, with all the wealth we have gotten from it, haven't we?"

He paused long enough that Lolly thought he wanted an answer. She had never turned her mind to where pepper or cotton or tea came from, so she didn't have an opinion herself. "I suppose so."

"A few of them lived in nice houses, I will admit that. But the majority were worse off than our commoners. It is not a true trade. Take cotton, for example. We don't export wheat to them as an exchange. We tell them that we need them to grow cotton; we loan them the seeds and equipment; then we take the cotton at such a low price they can't repay their loans. When they default, we give them no forgiveness. When there is a famine, they die, because they have used their fields for cotton, not food crops. When they steal because they are hungry, we punish them as the Company on behalf of the Crown."

With each sentence, he had increased his pace, as if speed would shake off his anger. Lolly had to hurry to keep up. "That doesn't sound Christian."

He barked something that might have been a laugh. "If only God had something to do with it, Lady Rosalind. Although I'm not at all sure He is on our side. After all, He saw fit for the American colonies to defeat us. I wonder if even now He is plotting the same for our other territories."

Lolly tried to think what to say next, but Lord Preston kept going.

"On my return voyage, we made several stops along the West African coast. In Ouidah, I saw a slaver trade one bolt of pink Indian muslin for two men. I already had reservations before, but it was in that moment that I resolved to have nothing to do with imports from the Indies. As if cotton could be equated with the value of a life."

Lolly flashed back to the escaped slave who had shown up in her friend Frances's kitchen in Boston. His eyes had been so full of fear, a fear that didn't completely disappear even as Frances's mother cleaned the wounds from his journey.

And in the same moment, her hand fell to her skirts, which were a soft, fine cotton.

"I thought it would be better when I returned to England. Surely, here we treat our kinsmen with kindness. But even at Northfield, your father would have me cut off my neighbors from their firewood and grazing grounds, in the name of improvements." Lord Preston came to a sudden stop. "You must forgive me if I have offended you. I am having trouble readjusting to English society, that is all."

He was incredibly endearing, staring down at her with anxiety lacing his every feature. A man like him – handsome, rich, powerful – so rarely looked anything other than sure of himself. But now, even his hair in its queue curled uncertainly about his neck. Lolly looped her arm through his, the better to reassure him. "Perhaps you are having trouble adjusting because you have, like me, discovered that English society is worse than no society at all."

Lord Preston looked down as if discovering her for the first time. "We cannot truly know what it is to have no society, can we? Especially not you and I. How would we eat? Clothe ourselves? Build shelter?"

They walked arm in arm. The pace was more civilized now. Lolly could feel every brush of his chest against her gloved hand. Every collision between his knee and her layered skirts. "I suppose I did not mean all of English society," Lolly answered. "Only the Quality. Anyone who is so consumed with proving that they are better than everyone else."

Lord Preston smiled. His smile was so very crooked. Lolly caught herself admiring it – and forced her gaze away.

He asked, "Did you acquire your dislike of norms in the American colonies? Or did you come to it on your own as a product of living in England?"

She supposed it did all trace back to Frances. "I would prefer to say I am a critical thinker, my lord. I do not dislike all norms. The norm of not murdering someone, for example, is a very good one."

"What of the norm of calling each other by such formal appellations? Can we dispense with that?"

Surprised, Lolly looked up to see if he was jesting. But he still smiled, perfectly serious and friendly. "Since we are not actually going to marry, would that be wise?"

"What would happen if you called me Martin? Would your virtue combust?"

She couldn't help laughing. "I am led to believe a hundred fierce matrons would rush forward with swords to defend me from such an act."

"Perhaps you should test your theory." He raised an eyebrow at her.

Lolly shouldn't flirt. Not with him, not with anyone, now that she had decided against marriage. Except it was too much fun. She couldn't help grinning back at him. "What do you think we shall eat for luncheon, Martin?"

It was a thrilling name, Martin. It called to mind a medieval knight who would fight dragons to free her from a prison tower.

"I daresay it will be a roast, Rosalind." He darted his eyes about the fields. "There, you see? No matrons out to get us yet."

"Call me Lolly," she corrected.

Martin set his dark, kind eyes on her. "If you insist, Lolly."

It was only when they didn't stop staring at each other for long moments that Lolly realized her mistake. They weren't marrying. Her skin wasn't supposed to tingle under his gaze. Her lips were not supposed to yearn for his.

Her heart wasn't supposed to skip this way.

Chapter Four

T HIS WAS HIS FAVORITE path. How many times, over the past five years, had he conjured it in his mind as a refuge from the stormy ocean crossings and hot deserts and overwhelming people?

Martin inhaled the smell of meadow grass and the sight of the hills rising in the distance. Everything was a little bit smaller and a little bit shaggier than he remembered. England had not sat still while he traveled. Even his own fields had changed, now growing tall with wheat instead of the rye they'd been harvesting at his departure five years ago. And this time, he walked with a pretty woman at his side.

That, at least, was an improvement over the last time he had been home.

The echo of her name resonated between them. He couldn't think of anything clever to say next, and as the silence grew longer, it morphed into something comfortable. Lolly looked about herself, taking in the fields and hills just as Martin had. He relaxed into the moment and enjoyed the walk to the pond.

The pond was one of Martin's favorite places in the whole world. Nestled at the conjoining dip of three farm fields, it hid from the horizon like a desert oasis. Long ago, the trees surrounding it had been removed, except for three old oak trees that refused to be felled. They offered just enough shade for soft green moss to blanket their roots. The pond itself always glimmered, even on the cloudiest day, and in the summertime, it beckoned with water warmed by the sun.

At the moment, the sky was gray, the air chilly enough to put cherries in their cheeks, and so instead of recommending a swim, Martin simply helped Lolly sink against one of the oak trees, then sat beneath the one he had, as a boy, christened The Holy Spirit.

"Welcome to my private office," he said, sneaking her another smile. "If ever you cannot find me at the hall, likely as not I am here."

"That would be good to know, were we to marry." Lolly sat straight as an arrow against the tree and surveyed the pond. "I can see why you like it. It is very peaceful here."

Martin settled into the place and moment, listening to the birds chirping above. Then, he asked the question that most pursued him. "What are you going to do instead of marriage, then? Convert to Catholicism and join a convent?"

"No." Lolly crossed her arms. Even though they were in the country, she wore padding underneath her dress so that her skirts billowed across the mossy ground.

Martin waited for her to say more. When she didn't, he prodded, "Don't you have any sort of plan?"

"I will return to Boston, where I will become a schoolteacher and charity worker." From the way she said it, Martin was not at all sure that she had formed this plan before opening her mouth.

Lord Turner had explained to Martin how his daughters had been born in Boston and that the family had only returned at the outbreak of the American war for independence. But Martin hadn't thought much of it; Lolly would have been a child when they returned to England, and it never occurred to him she would have loyalties there.

He was so taken aback that all he could find to say was, "I heard they don't even have paved streets in Boston."

She laughed. "Of course they have paved streets." Then, more soberly, she raised a pointed eyebrow at him. "Besides, I imagine they don't have paved streets in all the places you traveled to, but that didn't stop you."

"No, but I didn't plan to settle in any of those places." Though his brother had done, and very happily so, in a little village outside Calcutta. He swallowed down his next argument – besides, I'm a man – knowing it would only spark an argument. "Why not stay in London? Surely we need schoolteachers and charity workers as much as Boston does."

"My friend runs an institution for orphans in Boston. I will be joining her."

Martin tried to picture her in a severe gray headmistress's outfit. Would she scowl at her pupils? Hit them with a cane when they misbehaved?

He couldn't see anything except the spirited woman before him who was at that very moment struggling to stop a sneeze.

"What a pair we are. Instead of doing the sensible thing and marrying, I'm participating in subterfuge and you're off to fulfill your destiny helping orphaned children in Massachusetts."

She twigged her nose with a handkerchief. "And what exactly is your plan, anyhow? Throw all the cotton and sugar and tea you can find into the river in protest?"

The image was so absurd that he had to laugh. "The list is too long to fit in the river. You have forgotten silk, mahogany, Madeira, indigo, rum, tobacco…I scan the arrivals listed in the newspaper and constantly have another import to avoid."

Leaning forward – so close to him that he could smell her perfume – Lolly poked Martin's jacket. "Is this not silk?"

He had never noticed her hands before, but now he watched in slowed time as her finger curled back into its fist. How he wanted to catch it, to pull her palm against his and feel her skin.

Martin dragged his thoughts back to the conversation. "That's how difficult my proposition is. I must find a tailor who will provide me clothes in English linen and wool."

"I have never thought much about it," Lolly began, folding her skirts this way and then that in thought, "but I was under the impression all those goods you would throw in the river are a sign of prosperity. If you succeeded in ridding us of all we import, would we be plunged back into the time of knights?"

It was a question he had posed to himself a hundred times. But never had he been forced to vocalize his response, and all of a sudden, he found an actual answer. "Look at these fields. Right now, we use them to produce wheat, wheat, and wheat, not so that those of us who live here can consume it, but so that we can sell it off and earn a profit. Why not focus our improvements on growing the crops we need to care for ourselves, not to fulfill the market?"

He watched her in profile as she took in the fields. His response satisfied himself, but he was not at all sure that she would agree. He was not sure that anyone would.

Lolly turned her dark, solemn gaze to him. "How do you define 'we'?"

Not the rebuttal he was expecting. "Everyone, I suppose. Northfield Hall, of course, but also my tenants and the townspeople who rely on these commons."

She evaluated him silently for a moment. The breeze drifted between them, too cold to be comfortable. From one of the trees, a robin chirped.

Martin couldn't wait any longer under the weight of her gaze. "I doubt it will make a difference. They will say I've become an eccentric and ignore everything I say."

Lolly reached a hand towards him. It landed in the grass between them. "I suppose you must do what you can. Even if it feels that it isn't making a difference. You have already had an influence on me."

She was beautiful in her endless skirts and solemn gaze and red nose twitching with another sneeze. Martin wondered if all engaged couples spoke so openly with each other, or if he were lucky in the woman he had compromised.

He found himself staring at the little mole above her lip.

That would not do at all. "Luncheon will be served soon. We had better head back."

"I'm looking forward to the roast," Lolly smiled. She held out her hands, waiting for him to help her up. He pulled her to her feet with a little too much energy, and she stumbled against him. Her breasts pressed his chest for just a second. And oh, he was so aware of that second.

Martin's hands steadied her at the waist. Lolly was staring up at him with those warm eyes; uncertainty, something he had never before seen from her, widened her mouth.

He stepped back. "If I were your real fiancé, I would ask you for a kiss."

She grinned. "If you were my real fiancé, I would allow it."

And then, she turned and ran back towards the house.

Chapter Five

Lolly still hadn't written Frances.

For the last three mornings, she told herself that would be the day. It wasn't so complicated after all. She had been writing to Frances every month for years. Martin would post it for her; all Lolly had to do was put pen to paper.

Except she couldn't seem to make herself do it.

Explaining the situation would be tricky enough. Even though the encounter on the balcony had been as innocent as a lamb in May, when written out, it sounded ridiculous. *He knelt to free my skirts from the railing.* Lolly knew it sounded like a lie. And she flinched to think what Frances would make of it.

Then, once she sorted out that section of the letter, Lolly would have to ask Frances to take her in. Lolly knew with deep certainty that Frances would welcome her at the orphanage. But she worried that Frances would tell her not to come if it meant lying to her parents and fleeing a fiancé.

So another day passed without writing the letter, and then another, and Lolly grew increasingly anxious that she would never convince herself to do it at all.

Her penance was being trapped in Northfield Hall with her family. Louisa and Charlotte bickered over everything, including what color dresses they would wear at the wedding. Mama kept correcting Lolly on her posture, her language, and her behavior, as if she were still a girl of fourteen. Papa, meanwhile, was practically giddy, and he paraded around Northfield pointing to this and that which Martin could improve.

Now that she knew how Martin felt about Papa's suggestions, Lolly cringed whenever she heard them.

She thought about Martin's boycott often. Almost more than she worried about her letter to Frances. She knew the Quakers and a few eccentric ladies boycotted sugar on account of slavery. Mama had even purchased a sugar bowl painted with a little African boy in chains from a fundraiser for the Abolition Society. But Papa had scoffed when Mama showed him the dish: "As if porcelain will change the fundamentals of our economy."

Lolly had been satisfied with that analysis. Until now. Until Martin suggested with no trace of a smile that the entire system was base. Cruel. Perhaps even inhuman.

Now she wanted to think about it more. With the right person answering her questions.

And every time she contemplated it, she blushed with shame. Because as much as she wanted to learn more about Martin's theory, twofold did Lolly regret not letting him kiss her.

She had kissed Ned once, back when she thought he was going to propose. They were at a ball at their mutual neighbor's, the Pemberlys, and she had let Ned lead her down to the lake under the moonlight. "You're so beautiful," he had said, and then he had cupped her chin in his palm and kissed her.

It had been delectable. Unforgettable. Addictive.

Then Ned had turned around and married Ursula instead.

Lolly wondered what Martin's kiss would be like. Would he dart his tongue between her teeth the way Ned had? Would his hands wander beyond her chin? Would he taste of strawberries?

Would her body melt into another foolish puddle?

She knew she shouldn't want to kiss him. It was only proper for an engaged couple to kiss because they would soon have the protection of marriage. Whereas Lolly would be jilting Martin in a blink. What would Martin think of her, if she actually let him hold her?

It was unfair, really, that a woman was supposed to guard her virtue so viciously. Men enjoyed all sorts of escapades before marriage. All Lolly wanted was one little kiss.

Perhaps Martin wouldn't think badly of her at all. He always smiled so kindly at her. At the dinner table, he sought her opinion on topics, even when she wasn't seated beside him. When they passed in the corridors, he paused and asked her how her day was going.

All the expected behavior of a fiancé, of course. Each time it happened, Lolly resolved to ignore the burn of excitement across her skin.

But it did make her wonder about kissing him.

She was following her mother outside for an afternoon of embroidery in the quiet garden when Martin intercepted them. "Lady Turner, would you mind terribly if I stole Lady Rosalind away for a few minutes?"

Mama couldn't have been more pleased. "Certainly, my lord."

Lolly, curious, followed him down the main corridor and to the right, into the front room he used as a study. Other than a desk, it had little furniture or décor to advertise its function. At the moment, three large art canvases were spread across the floor.

"These just arrived from Portsmouth," Martin said, his voice husky with excitement. "I wanted to show you."

He led her around the perimeter of the room to face the door from the desk, so that she could look at the paintings from the proper angle. Unframed, the paint stopped not quite at the edges of the canvases. The blank margins filled Lolly with the same sense of embarrassment as if she had discovered Martin in his underclothes.

Not that she had any idea what that would be like. Or what he would look like.

She blinked to keep her focus on the oil paintings. One depicted a yawning green mountain range. Another looked out over a sea with little boats dotting the horizon. And the final was a never-ending field of cotton with bright blue sky above it.

"I had these commissioned from the Company School while I was in India," Martin explained. His brows were lifted in apprehension. "What do you think?"

"They are beautiful." Her neighbors the Pemberlys had a huge collection of Company School art, but most of it featured specimens of animals or sketches of intricate architecture.

"It is beautiful countryside. I can't tell you how many times our carriage would round a corner or come to the top of a hill and my jaw would drop into my lap in awe. And the whole Eastern world is colorful. Men, women, buildings. Everything is as colorful as it can possibly be." Martin pointed to the painting of the cotton field. "It took me a while to see the people in this one."

Lolly looked more closely. The cotton plants were painted in varying hues of brown with bright, white blossoms. Vibrant flowers peeked from between the bushes every now and then. Except when she examined it, she realized the flowers were people. Men dressed in colors dabbed with quick, tiny brushstrokes.

"If you are at a cotton field in truth, it is filled with laborers. No matter the season. They're either preparing the soil, planting, watering, or picking. If they don't tend the cotton, they won't be able to sell it back to us, and then they'll be in even worse debt." The excitement had drained from his voice.

Lolly ached after spending all of fifteen minutes trimming her mother's roses. She couldn't imagine doing it all day. Of course, the English would say that was because she was born into nobility. But

Lolly could hear Frances sneering at that. We're all God's children, not one of us made to be inferior to another.

Frances, to whom Lolly still had not written.

"What about the mountains?" Lolly asked. "Are they also hiding some unpleasant truth from me?"

She accidentally swayed closer to him with the question. Her shoulder brushed his, sparking a fire through her fingers to her core.

Martin didn't move as he pointed with his other arm to the first mountain scape. "I never visited those mountains, so I don't know anything beyond what I've heard, which is that it is desperately beautiful and remote." He shifted his hand to indicate the sea painting, and somehow he ended up leaning that much closer to her. "This one is the port where I first arrived. It is too treacherous for the ships to come into the harbor, so they anchor in the sea and little boats carry us to land in churning waves." Martin dropped his hand. "Anyhow, since you were kind enough to listen to me rant the other day, I wanted you to see a little bit of what I saw. I commissioned these paintings so I wouldn't forget. I was afraid when I returned to England, I would be lulled back into complacency by the silver-tongued rhetoric of my peers. These are to remind me of all I learned."

Lolly allowed herself a quiet, secret thrill that he had been thinking of her. Then she glared at the cotton farm to suppress the reaction. She was supposed to be indifferent to him. "Do you think it is possible to undo the harm our commerce has caused?"

He looked down at the same moment she tilted her chin up. His gaze was as intense as it was thoughtful, and Lolly had to look away.

"I think it is more like a gash in the arm." In a sudden movement, Martin seized her arm. His fingers feathered from the base of her wrist up, skating all the way to her elbow. "The wound cannot be removed entirely, but with the proper stitching, it can heal."

Lolly's breath froze in her lungs. Her mouth and hands and thoughts were dry. Her whole being was her left forearm, waiting – yearning – for what his fingers would do next. For a moment, she believed they were two beings suspended in time. And then he drew his fingers backwards, down the length of her sensitive skin, until he held nothing but her palm in his two hands.

His gaze clung to her again. "I do not know what the right thing to do is. That is where I equivocate. But I must do something. I am a lord of the realm. Is it not my responsibility, designated by God at birth, to see to those who are less fortunate than me?"

It was all Lolly could do to breathe, "Yes." She had never imagined passion could feel more potent – or pure. For a moment, all they did was stare at each other, hand in hand.

Then Lolly couldn't stand it anymore. She launched onto her tiptoes and pressed her lips to his.

M ARTIN NEEDED TO DO the right thing. In every circumstance. It was the drumbeat behind each step he took.

He wanted to do the right thing. Only Lolly's lips were so soft. She smelled of tea and biscuits. Her fingers dug five points into each of his biceps, and his whole body responded. Tongue against hers. Palms to her waist. Cock into the swell of her skirts.

This was the wrong thing. But it felt right. Natural. Perfect. Now her hands roamed downwards, flat against the sides of his jacket, drifting closer and closer to the tuck of his breeches. He brought his palms to her cheeks, reveling in the soft of her olive skin. He traced her jaw with his thumbs. She tasted so right. And she was his fiancée. And she felt perfect beneath his touch.

He wouldn't have pulled away, no matter the right thing, except someone nearby cleared their throat.

Martin practically threw Lolly across the room. His heart hammered, expecting to see Lord Turner, and he braced for a dressing down.

But it was Maulvi. His eyes were trained on the ceiling. "Shall I return later, my lord?"

It was just like him to gallop in as Martin's conscience. He had always been the one in the family to nudge Martin in the right direction, whether it was to mind his tutors or to write his mother more from London. Martin cleared his throat, as if that would straighten the rest of this mess out.

Lolly pressed a hand – which had so recently been measuring the expanse of his body – to her chest, as if to calm her heart. Her lips were swollen, her nose dotted the red of a cherry. At least her dress didn't need any fixing.

Martin's thoughts tripped over that last part. Could he really be so base? He had nearly defiled her, this woman who refused to marry him, and he was patting himself on the back for not mussing her dress?

She smiled at him. It was soft and secret and delicious, that smile.

If they were actually planning to marry, Martin could forgive his lust. But he knew Lolly would leave him. He knew she was going to venture into the world on her own; how could he dare make her mission harder as a fallen woman? He should never have touched her, much less kissed her.

"No, Mr. Maulvi." Martin's voice came out as a lash. "Please come in. Lady Rosalind, you will excuse us."

Lolly blinked at him. For a moment, her face still lifted with the smile. But then, upon his dismissal, it disappeared. She looked nothing except bereft. Ravished and bereft.

He was a right scoundrel. That was all that could be said.

Chapter Six

It took exactly one quarter of an hour for Lolly's embarrassment to crystalize into anger. Rejoining her mother and sisters in the garden, her eyes stung with tears. One moment, Martin had been caressing her with his tongue, and the next, he had banished her from the room. The look in his eyes as he did so, too – oh, Lolly couldn't stand how his whole body shimmered with disgust. She shouldn't have kissed him.

Lolly had not realized how much she wanted Martin's esteem. Even though she wouldn't marry him. He was handsome – that was part of it. But more, he tried so hard to be kind. To live up to the noble in nobility. He thought about the world so differently than anyone Lolly had ever met. She hadn't realized how much she wanted to absorb that. Or how much she wanted him to see the same qualities in her.

Instead, he looked at her with disgust.

That circle of thoughts kept flooding her eyes, so that she had to blink every few moments otherwise spear her fingers with the needle.

But as she revisited the incident in the study for the hundredth time – ignoring her sisters' endless debate on which slogan was better for a pillow cushion – the tears disappeared. No, she shouldn't have kissed him. But he had kissed her back. Not accidentally, either. His hands had known exactly where to go, his tongue exactly how to undo her, his hips… Lolly had felt his hard sexual organ even through the layers of her gown.

If Mr. Maulvi hadn't interrupted, Lolly suspected Martin would have kept kissing her. Perhaps he would have done more: touched her, undressed her, even swived her.

And he was the one who knew what all that was about. Lolly had kissed him out of pure instinct; she had only a vague idea of what came next. He was the gentleman. He was supposed to put a stop to such activities. Or at least warn her when they were about to go too far. For that matter, Martin was the one who had touched her first. The kiss was merely a natural reaction to him.

In which case it was himself he should be disgusted with, not her. He had no right to toss her across the room like a hot iron he shouldn't have touched. To glare at her, as if she were a snake that had slithered into his boot. He was the one leading her to temptation, not the other way around.

"Charlotte, really, you can't be serious!" Louisa interrupted Lolly's thoughts with a strident screech. "To thine own self be true? What will people think?"

"Not all pillows have to quote the Bible," Charlotte retorted, her voice thick with hurt.

"Oh yes they should!" Louisa gasped in the same moment that Mama said in her quiet ultimatum voice, "Young ladies!"

Lolly measured her feelings. She had run out of the study in such desperation. Heavy limbs, sinking stomach, stinging eyes. But now she felt only anger. Buoyant, hot, righteous anger.

It wasn't fair that Martin should shame her. Clearly, he wasn't the kind man she had thought him. And clearly, he wasn't as open-minded as she expected. After all, every lord was expected to "sow his wild oats" before marrying, a saying which Lolly knew referred to even more than kissing. Here she was, engaged to marry this man, and he wanted to shame her for claiming a kiss?

She jerked out of her chair. "Please excuse me, Mama."

Mama nodded, even as Louisa asked, "Where are you going?"

"I have to write to Frances." Lolly didn't even feel guilt as she lied, "To share the good news with her."

"Oh, Frances," Louisa sighed. "You put too much stock in her opinion, if you ask me."

"Frances was always too serious," Charlotte chimed in. Lolly swept past them, not bothering with a reply. There was one thing on her mind: to finally right this wrong engagement.

Maulvi raised an eyebrow at Martin as Lolly rushed out, then walked calmly to the baron's desk. "The list you requested, my lord."

Martin felt his face burning. "It's good you came. I had forgotten myself."

"I saw nothing." Maulvi did look amused though, with his lips hitched in a little smile. "Nothing that is inappropriate for a few months before the wedding, anyhow."

Except they weren't getting married. And he couldn't tell anyone, not even Maulvi. Martin hurled out a curse, then dropped to his knees to roll up the painted canvases. "You have always been my conscience, Maulvi. I am indebted to you for that. If only I could live up to your example."

Maulvi helped roll the third painting. It was a moment before he said, "That would mean more if you actually knew what kind of example I set."

Martin tucked the paintings into their cylindrical cases one by one. "Of course, I know your example. What, do you imply that you have been lying to me all these thirty years?"

"Not lying." Back on his feet, Maulvi arranged the papers on the desk into straight, careful lines. "I am your servant, nothing more."

Martin stared at the man. His skin still sang with the memory of Lolly, and now Maulvi wanted to confuddle things with another complication. Hang it. "You are my family. Nothing less."

There was one more moment of silence. Maulvi watched Martin tensely from the corner of his eye; Martin looked down, brushing his hands as if doing so could erase the last quarter hour. Not that he wanted to erase Lolly's kiss. Except, of course, he should want to do so.

"Let's see that list, then." It was a ledger of all the tenants who worked his fields as well as the known households in Thatcham who relied on the Northfield commons for pasture. Martin wanted to know precisely whom he would be cheating if he ever decided to take Turner's advice.

He tried to concentrate on it. He recognized most of the names, though he couldn't conjure faces for every family. His father had preferred Martin to stay in London and curry favor with the younger set of lords than to join in visits to the tenants. Martin couldn't even say for sure whether his father had done the visits himself or handed them off to Mr. Maulvi.

If he didn't know even that – something so simple – then perhaps Maulvi was right. "What kind of example do you set, then?"

Maulvi blinked at him. Martin had always envied the man his dark eyes, for it was almost impossible to tell whether his pupils widened in alarm or remained staid as ever.

"You charge that I do not know you," Martin pushed. Perhaps he shouldn't. He certainly wouldn't with any other servant. But Maulvi wasn't a servant, not precisely. Not in Martin's heart, anyway. "So tell me. What don't I know?"

Maulvi cleared his throat. "I have a sweetheart. In the village. The Widow Croft." He paused, as if expecting Martin to recognize the name. Martin tried to keep his expression completely neutral as he nodded cooperatively, although he had never heard of the woman. "We wanted to marry. But the vicar refused, since I am not Christian."

Martin hoped he showed no external reaction. He knew of Maulvi's religion, of course. Maulvi's parents had been brought back from India by his own grandmother along with a Manipuri pony, on account of Maulvi's father being an excellent horse trainer, and the little family had remained Muslim despite everyone's best attempts to baptize them. Martin hadn't guessed that a Christian woman might take up with a Muslim man. If he was being honest with himself, he had never much considered whether or not Maulvi wanted a wife of his own, no more than he wondered that about Mr. Hewett or the footman.

And yet he claimed to consider Maulvi family.

"Neither of us wants to convert to the other religion, and so we live in sin. Have done for seven years."

Martin had to look away. He simply couldn't keep a smile from his face, trying to imagine Maulvi arm-in-arm with a woman. It felt absurd and wrong; and that, itself, stacked bricks of guilt in his stomach.

He did consider Maulvi a family member. Then did this rude reaction indicate that Martin was a bad family member, or that Maulvi's circumstances truly did shade their relationship?

He realized something. "You and Widow Croft live in sin here at Northfield Hall?"

"No." Now Maulvi himself laughed. "Have you not seen me walking in every morning? I live with her at Thatcham."

Martin had seen Maulvi on the drive at godawful hours of the morning – right when Martin was stretching out of bed – but he had assumed the man was surveying the grounds. "You walk? That's more than five miles."

"I am used to it." He said this with the quiet confidence he usually used. Its return was the only reason Martin realized it had disappeared. For a moment there, Maulvi had been grinning, his voice exuberant enough to carry across the room.

Martin hated to see that version of him go. Particularly since he had only just discovered it. He thought of his father's horse, a fine thoroughbred standing around the stables all day. "Take Theseus today. And every day. Consider him a wedding present."

"My lord..." Maulvi stared at him. He opened and closed his mouth a few times, but he seemed to find no words.

"We are alone, Mr. Maulvi. You may call me Martin, or Preston, or Ashforth. You may even refer to me as Fool. But not 'my lord.'" When the other man still gaped, Martin said with finality, "As I said, we are family."

"Thank you. Martin." They both looked away at how strange it sounded. "You are too kind."

They returned to the list. Martin still couldn't quite concentrate. He would do better by Maulvi from here on out. He would put actions to his words. Show Maulvi just how much Martin valued him, not as a steward but as a person.

Now he kept thinking of Maulvi and the Widow Croft. It wasn't hard to imagine, once he accustomed himself to it. He was glad that Maulvi had someone lovely to go home to. Someone who put that foolish grin on his face.

And that led him back to Lolly. He should have smiled at her as they parted. There had been a moment – no longer than an instant – when he saw horror fill her eyes. Not because of the kiss, but because of how he reacted afterward. He shouldn't have behaved so. He shouldn't have kissed her, but neither should he have hurt her.

Martin didn't know how to fix it. And, with her jilting him, with her looking so delectable, with him knowing just how wonderful it was to kiss her, Martin didn't know if he should even try.

Chapter Seven

Martin didn't look at Lolly all throughout supper. She knew because she kept stealing glimpses of him. As she forked more roasted pike onto her plate. As she turned her head to respond to Louisa. As she nodded at the footman to refill her wine glass. And every time she did, his attention was fixed elsewhere. His conversation, too, remained stubbornly upon her father, coaxing out of Papa increasingly louder opinions on correcting the Poor Man's morals.

"It is not enough to force them to church. We have seen that over and over again. The only way the poor will ever learn is to fine them. Money is all the poor man seems to care about, God help us."

Lolly reached out to fix a candlestick to cover her look to Martin. He stared down at his plate, his jaw tense.

She had a rejoinder for Papa, one that would open the conversation towards Martin's general direction of thinking, but she hardly considered the man worthy of her help. So she returned her attention to the potato pie.

"Ah, Preston, I forgot to mention earlier that we have a surplus of clover seed at Macarius Abbey. I will have my man send some over so that you can start it on your fields. I vow, in no more than two years, you'll see your profits triple."

It was embarrassing, now that Lolly knew how much Martin disagreed with her father, to hear Papa spouting these theories. Worse was that Lolly agreed with Martin, though she knew so little about the topic. The profit her father spoke of would come at the expense of the villagers – and the tenants who couldn't keep up with the new crops. The very people that the barony was supposed to ward.

She thought of the letter to Frances, burning a hole in her pocket as she waited to dispatch it. She had finally stilled her thoughts long enough to write it.

I have spent these last eight years as a dutiful daughter to a dutiful earl. What I have learned – what the brave men who lead your United States already know – is that the aristocrat's duty is not to the welfare of his people, but rather to the welfare of his own reputation and coffers. My dear Frances, how can I allow myself to continue this terrible legacy?

It wasn't a lie. It truly was what had pounded through her head ever since her walk in the fields with Martin.

But it wasn't quite the truth either.

The party broke up informally after supper. Mama cried off from the drawing room on excuse of a headache. Louisa declared she had no use for card games and pulled out her sketchpad in a corner of the room, while Charlotte dreamily stared out the window. Lolly had resigned herself to picking up a book when Martin responded to Papa's invitation for a smoke with, "You'll excuse me, Lord Turner. I would have a moment of Lady Rosalind's time, if you will permit it."

"Of course. She is your problem now, after all," Papa chuckled. One hand on Lolly's back, he pushed her towards Martin.

She smoothed on a simpering smile. "Anything you wish, my lord."

They went out into the garden again, although this time Martin did not lead her out the back gate. Papa closed the door behind them against the brisk night air. "I leave her in your hands, Preston."

It was disgusting, really, how happy Papa was to foist her onto this man. She knew he believed them to be in love, but that was only because he refused to listen to the truth of what happened on that London balcony.

In any case, she decided going on the offensive was her best choice. Withdrawing the letter from her pocket, she held it out to Martin. "Would you please post this for me, when you get a chance?"

Taking it, he looked at both sides of the envelope suspiciously. "What is this?"

"A letter to my friend in Boston to arrange my arrival."

They marched along the path in silence for a few moments.

"I must apologize for my behavior earlier today." Martin's voice was quieter than usual. Lolly almost felt the night breeze would steal his words away. "I have no excuse, but I beg your forgiveness."

She had an instant reaction, and it was anger. She breathed in, repeating his words in her mind, to dampen it. Although really, his apology was as bare as her father's bald spot. On her exhale, she molded her voice into that of a lighthearted lady. "For which behavior are you apologizing, precisely? The kiss, or tossing me across the room at first sign of interruption?"

"I don't know that I tossed you –"

"My neck still aches from the impact."

Martin tipped his head towards the stars. He really was too handsome. One could get wrapped up in the perfect resonance of his features and miss the fact that he was a flawed man.

Lolly looked away.

"I apologize for both. Kissing and tossing. I should have done neither. I am ashamed of myself."

"Of yourself? I find that hard to believe. Your behavior made it clear you were ashamed of one person in that room, and it was the female who dared kiss her fiancé." The words flew out her mouth before she could consider them. Or stop them. "And, if I may be honest, it is precisely that type of attitude that makes me eager to leave Society. I'm sure that wasn't your first kiss. I'm sure you have even done the marital act before, despite being unmarried your whole life. And yet it is I whom you blame."

She glared at the row of lettuce rather than watch for Martin's reaction. She didn't want to see indignation or outrage or shock. She didn't expect much of a response, truthfully, except one that would set in her in her place. One that would make it easy to sail to Boston.

"You speak honestly, and so now let me. I do not blame you, and I am sorry that I made you feel that I do." Pausing, Martin bent, pulled up a weed from the garden bed, and then resumed walking. "However, I am not sure I follow your logic. Biology dictates that a woman who engages in...the marital act, as you call it...is at risk of growing with child, while a man runs no such risk. Therefore, the woman must guard her chastity much more closely."

Lolly nearly laughed at his absurdity. "Biology dictates that the man is at risk of impregnating a woman. Should that not come with the same caution that the woman is supposed to exercise?"

"It's not that simple. There are different types of women."

"Oh, just as there are different types of men? Those who toil in the fields and those who rule them?"

"In a way."

Her arms crossed her chest, as if her subconscious knew she needed a shield. "Yet you would do away with those divisions between men."

"I have no objection to the divisions. Those of us born into nobility are better disposed to leadership, and those born into farming are better disposed to farming. What I would do away with is the unequal balance of power and wealth."

"Fine, then. I would do away with the unequal balance of responsibility between the man and woman – no matter her class. If you have the right to plunder women outside of marriage, then I should, at the very least, have the right to kiss my fiancé before our wedding day."

Somehow, they had turned to face each other. Martin's expression was outlined by a mixture of the moon and the spill of candlelight from the drawing room. It was a study of shadows and planes, fierce glittering eyes, and lips. Lolly couldn't look away from his lips.

"The flaw in your logic," he said, "is that I know you do not intend for there to be a wedding day."

She drew her eyes upwards, painfully. "Perhaps if you had thanked me for the kiss, I would have changed my mind."

Now their gazes were locked. Lolly felt a contest, as if whoever looked away first admitted weakness. But underneath that, a different kind of pressure built. A sizzle in the air between them. A quickening of her breath. A tingling in her fingertips and lips and hips. The urgent need to touch him and be touched and feel the world disappear again, the way it had that afternoon.

She thought he might be about to kiss her when Mr. Maulvi interrupted – again.

"My lord, may I have a word?"

M ARTIN HAD LOST TRACK of everything except Lolly. It could have been the middle of the day or spitting snow pellets; they could have been totally alone or surrounded by a thousand onlookers; he could only say that Lolly stood before him in a pink silk dinner gown threatening to marry him after all.

She wielded it like a threat, anyway, couched in the past tense until he agreed with her about the rights of women.

At that moment, he would have agreed to anything – even to a lifetime of picking cotton in India – if Lolly would marry him.

"My lord?" Mr. Maulvi said again, and the world crashed back into place. The dark of dusk, the chill in the air, the aroma of spring plantings. And Lolly turning away from him, already looking at his secretary.

Maulvi stood at the gate that led from the garden into the northern fields. He had changed from his elegant suit into simple trousers and sturdy boots, what Martin realized were his travel clothes.

He couldn't imagine what would be so important that Mr. Maulvi would interrupt at this hour, which only made his stomach twist with greater fear. Whatever the reason, it wasn't for polite company. "Please excuse me," he said to Lolly, putting enough pressure on her shoulder to orient her towards the house.

She trotted after him instead, stopping just behind him as he approached Mr. Maulvi. It was only when they got to the gate that Martin spotted the other two people, and he tensed instinctively at the surprise, splaying out his elbows as if that could protect Lolly.

It was a man and a woman, with the distinctive Eastern features of China or Singapore. The woman boasted a huge belly; she was perhaps only days from giving birth, with a swollen face and neck to match. The man had his arm around her, as if his grip was the only thing keeping her on her feet. They both wore simple clothes and kept their eyes averted.

"I came across Mr. and Mrs. Chow on the road to Thatcham. They are looking for work. I thought perhaps Mr. Chow could join the gardeners and Mrs. Chow could join the household." Mr. Maulvi stopped, almost as if tripping over what he had been about to say. His eyes roved to Lolly, whom Martin could feel beside him.

Martin prodded, "Mr. Hewitt could surely handle that."

"Mr. Hewitt turned them away."

Now Martin understood Maulvi's hesitation – and his urgency. Mrs. Chow could hardly walk back to town in her state.

"On what grounds?" Martin feared he already knew. There were not many Chinese in Berkshire, and Mr. Hewitt's specialty was instilling order, not being open-minded.

Mr. Maulvi glanced at Lolly again before answering. "He had several objections. Among them that the Chows were in the employ of Viscount Folkestone until a few months ago, when he discovered her condition, and have been essentially vagrants ever since."

The Chows stood so still that Martin could feel the fear emanating from them. He would have accepted them on the spot, except for what Lolly had just said. She might marry him after all. And he didn't know how she felt about hiring servants so objectionable that the head butler turned them away.

Lord Turner's baritone drifted through the window as he lectured at his daughters: "Curse the Englishman who shows more care for the East than he does for the opinion of Parliament."

Mrs. Chow swayed a little, and her husband's knuckles went white to keep her standing.

Lolly surged against Martin, her voice a hot, urgent whisper. "What are you waiting for? Can't you see she needs rest? Give them somewhere to sleep!"

It was no great act of charity. Had they been of the parish, any lady of the land would have offered them rest before showing them to the vicar for assistance. But Lolly's insistence rang all the way down to the depths of Martin's soul. That he could find a woman who would see the world as he did. That he could end up betrothed to her. That she might choose to wed him after all.

Martin gave Mr. Maulvi the necessary instructions to tuck Mr. and Mrs. Chow into a comfortable room amongst the servants. He offered them the shortcut through the garden to the servant's entrance. He ordered a hot meal served to their rooms. But the whole time, he felt Lolly behind him. And as soon as Mr. Maulvi led the Chows inside, he whirled around to grab her. She was tiny in his hands, nothing but hot flesh and cool silk. He pressed her against the brick wall and – before she could protest – kissed her the way he should have that afternoon.

"Is this what you want, then?" He scraped his lips along the side of her neck. "Is this the equality you demand?"

The gasp he got in response was not one of shock or surprise but pure, female delight. Her fingers weaved through his hair as his attention returned to her mouth. She tasted like hot, needful desire. There was nothing innocent about the way she thrust her tongue against his or nipped his lower lip between her teeth, and Martin's whole body responded. He pressed closer, his cock nestling against her soft thigh; even through the cushioning of petticoats, the touch was insanity, scattering his thoughts to nothingness.

Lolly's fingers tightened in his hair to guide his head downwards to her breasts. They were on display, as per fashion, in the low cut of her dress and the helpful push of her corset. All evening he had avoided them, afraid that once his eyes landed there, they would never pull away. Now he feasted. Lolly's guidance forced his lips to them. He tasted her bare skin, tracing his tongue along the edge of her bodice, languishing on the rises just above her nipples. The little moan that escaped her vibrated against his lips, and he felt it in every nerve ending. He pushed closer against her, his cock slipping now to the valley of skirts between her legs.

There was a part of him that still knew this was wrong. But Martin could barely hear it. Lolly wanted this, whether she married him or not. He wanted this. It had to be the right thing. She was the woman for him, whether their fate lasted these ten minutes or ten decades.

His lips returned to hers, drinking in the taste of her want, reveling in how she massaged her body against his. She needed him as much as he needed her; there was no better feeling than that. Still kissing her, he gathered her skirts in his two hands, drawing them up to her waist. He was about to repeat the action with her petticoats when the drawing room door opened.

"Time to come in now, Rosalind," Lord Turner called. "You'll get a chill."

They stood to the far right of the door, and an ornamental potted tree acted as a screen so they were not within direct eyesight. But barely. If Lord Turner cared to turn his head and squint, he would clearly see his daughter against the wall.

The man did not turn his head. "Yes, Papa!" Lolly called. "We'll return directly." After Martin released her, she smoothed her skirts, as if that could hide the desirous fever in her eyes or the red swell of her lips. For his part, he looked away, reciting French conjugations to erase the evidence of his cock. Lolly walked ahead of him on the path, smiling to her father as she reached the door. "We lost all thought of time to the philosophy of equality."

Lord Turner was not fooled; he smiled indulgently at Lolly and leveled Martin with a more sober glare.

Martin found he didn't care whether Lord Turner disapproved. He really didn't care for anything other than what Lolly thought. "Thank you for the discussion, Lady Rosalind. Have I successfully changed your mind?"

She looked back at him with a smirk. "I'm sure I cannot say until I have given it more thought." And she sauntered inside.

Chapter Eight

Northfield Hall was the type of house that grew deathly quiet at night. Wrapped in her quilt on the first story, Lolly could hear the creaks of servants closing up each room, the slow footsteps of her father retiring to his suite, the groan of the floorboards as everyone settled for the night. And then...nothing. With the thick curtains tied shut across the windows and brick walls closing her in, the house went silent. After a while, she couldn't even hear the crackle of the fire, seeing as it had cooled to embers.

It hadn't bothered her the other nights. She had fallen asleep almost as soon as tucking herself into a cocoon of covers.

Tonight, however, her whole body buzzed, as if it were midday instead of midnight.

What a day it had been. Burning anger at Martin, bookended by two unforgettable kisses. The last one in the garden had felt endless, like a bursting glimpse of eternity.

Even now, she felt the ghost of his lips exploring her skin.

He was only a few rooms away from her. This had always been true, but tonight, Lolly felt it as if he were lying on the mattress beside her. Separated only by a few walls and several hundred feet, Martin slept. She imagined him on his back, just like she was. Except he wouldn't turn to covers for comfort. He would be sprawled, two powerful legs stretching towards the bedposts. It was a warm enough night that perhaps he wouldn't be wearing anything except his nightshirt.

Maybe he would have removed even that.

Lolly pressed her eyes closed, a wave of hot desire rolling deep inside her. She shouldn't, but she couldn't help picturing him naked. She had felt his muscles beneath his clothes just hours earlier. His chest would be strong and firm, a canvas waiting to be kissed. His arms would flex as they reached above his head. And his legs...

Lolly had never properly seen a man's legs without trousers, but she remembered how they had felt pressed against her thighs, fully clothed. Strong. Demanding. With specific ideas of what might happen next.

There was his member, too. It was cloudy in her imagination, but that didn't matter. Again, she remembered its silhouette, nudging between her legs. She hadn't expected that to be so blinding, not with bolts of material between them. But the memory of it alone drove her fingers down to her quim. She rubbed her thumb against the point that always begged for attention. She imagined it was Martin, as eager for her as she was for him. She pressed herself against the mattress the way he had pressed her against the wall. She conjured his teeth nibbling at her neck. And while her thumb pulsed against her peak, her fingers slid downwards, charging all the way down to her channel. She made herself gasp, imagining it was Martin in all his male glory. Her daydream got bigger, looser, turning him into a shadow above her, kissing her as he pounded her, and before she even wanted to, she lost control, arching against her palm in white-hot pleasure.

She drew her hand back, trembling. She always did extra prayers the morning after nights like this. Begging forgiveness. Hating her body for coating her fingers with such wet, wanton desire. Wondering if she was the only deviant.

But it felt so right whenever she gave in. Natural. Her mind disappeared into her body; her body seized her mind.

Although neither did it feel like enough. She always wanted more: more time, more pressure, more fingers gathering inside of her. She didn't know exactly what marital relations would feel like, but she imagined it was what she did to herself, only better. More intense. More meaningful. More beautiful.

Martin had all but admitted to engaging in relations before, even though he wasn't married. He didn't have to waste hours in the night, wondering about the act. Worrying about whether, by choosing not to marry, he was sacrificing the opportunity to experience it. Worrying whether his life would stretch into loneliness without it.

It was a horrible reason upon which to make a decision. But there was a part of Lolly that was tempted to marry Martin only because it would mean she could finally experience the act. And hopefully experience it more than once. Whereas if she fled to Boston, she was good as committing her virtue to God. She couldn't ask Frances to give her a position with children and then turn into a fallen woman. She would have to be a paragon example of all good behavior.

If only she could experience the one time. Get it out of her system, so that it didn't hover over her decision. Then she could choose between a life with Martin or a life on her own, without her current haze of lust.

Her fingers had stopped trembling, but the rest of her body hadn't calmed yet. Rather the opposite: the heat between her legs felt more liquid than ever, and each nerve pounded against her skin, yearning for someone's touch.

He was only a few rooms away.

It was insanity, what Lolly was thinking of. It was abandoning all principles of good behavior and chastity. It was declaring herself loose and undeserving of respect.

She did it anyway.

Wearing nothing more than her nightgown, wrapper, and cap, Lolly tiptoed down the corridor. The silk carpet felt sinful beneath her toes. Near the landing, a floorboard squealed in protest at her weight, and she hurried into the shadow of the grandfather clock. But no one stirred.

Her heart raced in a thrilling, unstoppable way. Now Lolly moved faster. She fairly raced down the western wing, past family portraits and closed doors and a drafty window encasement. When they had first arrived, Martin had pointed out his suite – flushing behind his ears, Lolly remembered – and now Lolly slipped into it without even knocking.

She entered the sitting room. The drapes had not been drawn, and so moonlight spilled onto dark, oblong shadows that she assumed was furniture. To her left, the orange light of a fire framed another door.

Lolly almost turned back. This was bold – too bold. He had not invited her here. She was a thief, only instead of stealing from him, she was imposing upon him. Thrusting her honor at him. He might not want it.

He might turn her away in horror.

She didn't know why she kept going. It was like the morning after the balcony all over again, when her mouth had refused to say what she knew she must. Only then, her "no" had surged up from some inner well of stubbornness.

Tonight, her feet moved forward as if pulled by a magnet. As if she knew, even before opening the door, that Martin would be standing at his washstand, waiting for her.

Every grain of her body liquified at the sight of him.

He wore nothing but loose cotton drawers that hung from his hips to just below his knees. He held a washcloth to his shoulder. His chest glowed yellow in the firelight. His hair looked black and curled loosely down his neck. His lips parted in surprise at seeing her, but otherwise he was still, tense, coiled as if ready to pounce.

As she watched, a single droplet of water trailed from the washcloth, down the ridge of his chest, along his rippling stomach, and below the band of his drawers.

"What are you doing in here?"

It took her a moment to find words. "I have not changed my mind yet."

"This is my bedchamber."

"I am tempted to marry you only because I want to have relations with you." The phrasing sounded immature in the air. "Because I want you to swive me."

Martin's gaze trailed down her body. He said nothing.

"That would be the worst reason to make such a decision. Don't you agree?"

"You want me for my body." Martin's eyes held Lolly's now. Dark, smoldering coals that reflected her desire right back at her. "And nothing else."

Lolly had to swallow to bring moisture back to her mouth. He was close, close enough to smell, close enough to feel the shape of his words against her skin. It drove all reason from her mind.

"I don't know. I won't know, until I have..." He cocked an eyebrow. "...swived you."

"That isn't how it is done." Martin's voice came out huskily. "I wouldn't be doing right by you."

Her mouth opened of its own accord. "What is right? What Society dictates, or what is fair and kind and equal?"

Never during her stolen moments of pleasure had Lolly imagined discussing moral philosophy with her lover. But this was Martin. He did nothing without first weighing its moral impact.

It was why she wanted him in the first place.

"You want me to fuck you." The word flashed between them, hot and daring and right. "And then you might still leave."

"Don't I have the right to experience it once, before fixing the course of my life based upon whether I want to pledge my body to you or not?"

Martin reached forward and, one pin at a time, removed her sleeping cap. Her hair tumbled down. She felt a tendril brush her left nipple through the nightgown; she shivered.

The words between them had disappeared. His eyes roved over her. She didn't feel measured; she felt consumed. And she wanted to replace his gaze with the weight of his fingers. With the curiosity of his tongue. With the heat of his body.

Martin turned away. Silent, he dipped his washcloth in its basin and wrung it out. The excess water dripped loudly against the porcelain. Lolly's body strained under impatience. She needed him to touch her. But she didn't dare interrupt, not even as he took long moments to fold the cloth into a perfect square.

Finally, he looked at her again. He closed the distance between them so that they nearly touched. He smelled of a long day; Lolly resisted the urge to inhale it in gulps. She watched his eyes, opaque as they were. Without touching her, he pressed the cloth into her palm.

It was warmer than she expected.

"I was in the middle of washing," Martin said, his voice nothing more than a scrape now. "Finish for me."

For a moment, Lolly didn't understand. She wanted a swiving, not to be his nursemaid. He caught her hand and pressed it against his chest. The washcloth splayed between them. That was when she caught the flare in his eyes. The break in his breath. And she understood.

This could be so much more than she had even imagined.

LUST WAS THE SAME no matter in which country one found oneself. In Martin's experience, it changed depending on one's object, and he had never found a lightning rod quite like Lolly before.

He had been so hard after their garden escapade that he'd had no choice but to excuse himself early. Even a finger of scotch and an hour spent reviewing an agricultural magazine hadn't reduced the problem. And so, after the household turned in for bed, Martin had taken himself in hand. He tried not to imagine Lolly, tried not to think of the swell of her breasts in his palms or the taste of her lips or her little sounds of delight, but it had been an image of her face screwed into pleasure that had ushered his orgasm.

And then, not five minutes later, the lady herself walked into his bedroom.

She was breathtaking. He had always found her so, but especially now, wearing nothing except her nightclothes and insistence. He was halfway back to an erection from her words alone.

But not quite. And he thought perhaps – by the slimmest margins – if he could delay for even a few minutes, his mind could settle the matter once and for all.

He had to close his eyes so that he wouldn't see the desire pooling in hers as she dragged the washcloth across his skin. The water started warm, like the trail of a kiss, but went cool quickly, which helped keep his cock in cooperation. Martin tried to direct his thoughts with the washcloth: as she drew it down, he thought of his responsibility as a gentleman to guard her virtue; as she swept it back up, he wondered whether society had any right to dictate about her virtue. Her argument had several flaws, though at the moment, he couldn't quite articulate them. He knew she was neglecting the risk of pregnancy, but if she really meant to fuck him just the once, he could protect her against it.

She was assuming her lust would disappear after the one experience. That their bodies wouldn't keen towards each other in search of more and more and more. He should warn her of that. If she really wanted to make this decision without the mask of desire, she would do better to sail to Boston and decide from there.

But as to who had the right to decide how a woman should handle her virtue, Martin couldn't decide. Couldn't concentrate. Lolly's spare hand braced his back, below his ribcage, and the washcloth was descending towards his drawers.

He wanted her. But did he have the right to?

Then Lolly pressed her lips, open-mouthed, to his skin, just above his waistband. Her tongue swirled against the trail of hair.

Martin's eyes popped open as his cock stirred. Lolly had dropped to her knees. Her hair tumbled about her shoulders; before he could help it, he laced his fingers through its soft, endless locks.

He had always gone hard for a beautiful head of hair.

She smiled, the grin of a woman who knew just what she wanted. In a few quick gestures, she dropped both the washcloth and his drawers to the floor.

Martin was glad his cock was still recovering, otherwise he might have let her put her mouth around it. That was no way to satisfy her, not when he had only this night to change her mind. To convince her that she should marry him, no matter the circumstances of their engagement.

It gave him an idea, though, a compromise that would answer her desire without being entirely the wrong thing to do.

Catching her under the shoulders, Martin pulled Lolly into the air. She squealed and her eyes flashed, her hands landing on his bare shoulders. On the other side of the room, he tossed her onto the mattress. Her breasts bounced beneath her nightgown as she landed, and he nearly did it again just to relish the movement. Instead, he undressed her. He added extra force as he untied her wrapper and yanked it from her shoulders, watching as her whole face crumpled in need. He ripped her flimsy nightgown in two, just to see the near-orgasm ripple across her body.

"Yes," she breathed, her legs wrapping around his hips, "take me like a barbarian. Ravish me. I want you to."

Martin kissed her. He used his tongue and teeth and pressed his fingers hard into her wrists, as if he were punishing her. She whimpered in delight.

"Just like that," she whispered. "Oh, don't ever stop."

Another idea. Straddling her hips, Martin reached for the wrapper belt he had just removed and bound her wrists above her head in soft, tight knots. The nightgown became a blindfold. "Is that barbarian enough for you?" he growled into her ear.

"Take me," she moaned back.

Martin dismounted the bed just to admire his handiwork. Lolly lay on her back, completely nude. Her breasts were alive with desire, pert and round and begging to be suckled. She had spread her legs so he could see the brownish pink of her quim.

If he played the next half hour right, he could delight in this woman for the rest of his life.

"Martin," she said, twisting her head blindly. "Why are you making me wait?"

He had never been one for games in the bedroom. He preferred conversation to flirtation, and more to the point, he preferred serious women to the ones who needed flirtation to get into bed.

But there was an electricity in the air tonight. Perhaps because he admired Lolly so greatly. Perhaps because she knew so desperately what she wanted. He sensed without thinking what she needed.

And he wanted to give it to her.

Returning to the bed, he whispered an order against her ear. "Don't make a sound, unless it is to tell me how much you like something."

He followed his own desire first. With each breast cupped, he flicked his tongue across one, then the other nipple. "Yes, that, I like that," she breathed, and Martin settled in on the left. With his right fingers, he squeezed the other nipple hard, enough that she cried out. But she followed that with, "I like that even more."

Her breasts were perfect. He could have stayed with them all night, worshipping the areolas as they grew darker in pleasure. But he waited only until Lolly's hips were bucking, her quim instinctively rubbing against his thigh.

Then he continued his journey downwards. Her stomach tasted slightly sweeter than her breasts, and near her navel, he discovered a trio of moles that matched the one on her lip. He kissed each one, eliciting an eddy of breath from her, before nestling himself between her legs.

There was nothing like the feeling of a woman's knees hooked over one's shoulders. One's face directly confronting her most precious parts. Lolly smelled of desire. Her curls were even darker than her hair and already slick with juice. Martin admired them for a moment, trying to center his mind, to memorize this in case he never saw it again.

"Why aren't you inside me?" Lolly asked. "I want to feel you."

He bit at her inner thigh – gently – in response. "A barbarian doesn't care what you want."

"Oh."

Martin ran a finger between her folds. She jerked in surprise, then settled back down. He did it again, with more pressure this time, and hovered over her little hill. It was already stiff and engorged, more than his poor cock, and he nearly groaned at the feel of it.

"Yes." He could hear her words evaporate in the air, dissolving into pure pleasure. He bit at her thigh again as he looked for the right rhythm, starting slow, then going faster, then slowing again, until finally, Lolly said, "Whatever you do, don't stop."

It was mesmerizing, watching her skin respond to his touch. The way her quim seemed to breathe in sync with her lungs. He only wished he could kiss her mouth as he did this; his free hand drifted to his cock at the thought of it. He was hard again.

But that was neither here nor there.

"I know it has been forever, but keep going." Lolly said on a sigh. Her thighs tightened around his head. "Oh, keep going."

Martin wouldn't stop, not even with his wrist cramping. He ran his jaw along the soft side of her leg, letting his stubble raise her nerves, and she let out a cry of delight.

He didn't mean to stop, but he couldn't keep his mouth from her any longer, and suddenly he found himself cupping her quim with his tongue. She gasped. Lolly tasted just as he had imagined, soft and salty and delicious. Her mons leapt to his tongue. He caressed it, then grew rougher, faster, as her hips started shaking. When he couldn't take it anymore, he slid his index finger inside her canal and pulsed it firm and deep at the same time as licking her mons with all his might.

Lolly's body lifted into the air as she let out a great gasp of pleasure. It was so sudden that it knocked Martin backwards; he almost cut his lip on his own teeth. And just when he thought she was done – when he thought the display couldn't get any better – her orgasm turned into a loud, obnoxious sneeze.

She fell back into the mattress. Rolling beside her, Martin lifted the blindfold from her eyes, then untied the binding at her wrists. Lolly lifted her hands to his face, framing his cheeks in her palms.

"I had no idea it would be like that."

There was a fondness in her eyes; Martin's heart leapt with hope. "Did it change your mind?"

But she was in the stars. "I have never felt anything like that. It was better than I imagined. It didn't even hurt!"

The words didn't register with Martin until she reached down, touching herself, and examined her fingers.

She looked at him in confusion. "I didn't bleed at all?"

And Martin realized that, with the blindfold on, she thought he had entered her with his full staff.

That he had taken her virginity, just as she had asked.

"I only used my finger." He held up the offending digit. "You didn't think that my cock was that small, did you?"

The pleasure leeched from Lolly's face. "But I wanted to experience the marital act."

A myriad of answers crossed Martin's mind. For one, he hadn't meant their interlude to end just now; it was only a pause as she recovered from what he hoped was earth-shattering pleasure.

But there was also the fact that he had not, in fact, agreed to take her virtue before marriage.

He took too long to choose a response.

"No matter." Putting on her minx grin, Lolly vaulted to her knees. She wrapped his cock in two fists. "The night is hardly over."

The pressure was so much – too much – at once. Martin gasped, his vision going black. He reached blindly to remove her hands.

Lolly kissed him on the lips. "I want to be the barbarian now. I am anxious to have my way with you."

Even as he kissed her back, he dislodged himself from her grip. He guided her hands to his shoulders. "Why must it be the whole act? Haven't I already shown you the pleasure I can bring you?"

Lolly smiled in response. "I want to feel you inside me. I want to know how big a cock is inside me. I want to know how different that is from your mouth or your fingers." Lazily, she drew her own index finger along the ridge of his lips, then dipped it into his mouth.

He couldn't help but loop his tongue over it.

Her other hand wrapped back around his cock. "Besides, you need release, I can tell. I want to give you the pleasure you've already given me."

He wanted it. Of course, he wanted it. Most of Martin's being had been superseded by his cock at this point, and it all twitched needily under her touch.

Except for the one part of him that still drifted independently. The part that said he wasn't ready to cross this line.

He wished he didn't have to listen to it. He wished that for once, he could be the kind of man who ravished his fiancé when she showed up half-naked in his room at midnight.

Unfortunately, he was himself.

"I don't want to do this, Lolly."

She held onto his cock even as she blinked at him in confusion. "What is the difference between what we have already done and what remains to be done?"

"Pregnancy. Virtue. Honor." Martin tried to remove her hand. He couldn't think straight – much less be verbal – in her grip. But at his prodding, she only tightened her fingers.

"Hang your honor. I am telling you I want this."

"And I am telling you that I do not."

She held onto him for a moment longer. She glared at him. He merely stared back, willing her to let go. He had never feared someone forcing him to come when he did not want to; the strange possibility whistled an alarm in his head until finally, Lolly released him.

She scrambled backwards in the bed, collecting her assorted clothing as if to protect herself from him. "It is not for you to decide the right time for me to have marital relations."

So they were back to formal language. Martin reached for a pillow to cover his own offending nudity. "It is not for you to decide when I must reevaluate my ethics."

"Oh, I mustn't even suggest you could be wrong? Are you planning to wait until the entire House of Lords decides they must reevaluate their ethics on the economy, then? I thought you had a plan to change their minds."

Martin sighed. He hadn't meant to offend her. Or make her angry. He had only wanted to listen to his own conscience. "Lolly, I haven't had any time to think on this. I find you wildly attractive. Were we married, I wouldn't let you sleep tonight for all the ways I would bring you pleasure. But we are not married. And so I have a choice: break my honor tonight and wake up regretting it, with no recourse to undo my actions; or disappoint you tonight and hope you respect my honor enough to marry me anyway."

She looked away. The fire was burning low, and Martin could barely even make out her profile.

Her words, however, were clear enough. "So you choose to lose me and keep your precious honor."

There was perhaps a moment then when, if he had given the proper response, she would have let him touch her again. But Martin didn't say anything, and Lolly fled the room.

As he watched her go, he fancied he could hear his own heart break.

Chapter Nine

Lolly awoke to a dream – no, a memory – of Martin's hands drifting up her thighs. For a moment, she believed him in the room with her, saying something she couldn't quite hear. Something she desperately wanted to hear.

With consciousness came reality. What she heard was not Martin, but the sound of her parents arguing in the other room. Their disagreements were always conducted in hoarse, shouting whispers, as if the only rule they obeyed was to not raise their voices. And yet, as quiet as they tried to be, their words always carried, and Lolly and her sisters made a sport of eavesdropping.

"It is disgraceful. The woman is about to give birth! In the house where he proposes that Rosalind become mistress?" her mother shout-whispered.

"It will be a mark of dignity that they can afford foreign servants," Papa countered.

"If he had imported them directly! Not picked them off the highway like some common vagabond! Why, they could slit Lolly's throat at night while she is sleeping and run off with her jewels!" Mama heaved a dramatic sigh. "You must not let it stand, Albie. You cannot."

Lolly's first reaction was relief: they didn't know she had snuck into Martin's room the night before. But then her stomach twisted. It was obvious as day they were discussing the Chows. Although discuss was hardly the right term. It was hateful, what Mama said. And the worst part was that when Lolly had first spied Mr. Chow standing silently behind Martin's secretary, her own heart had leapt in fear.

But the Chows were no more criminals than they were a set of porcelain smuggled in on the wrong ship. Poor Mr. Chow was merely a husband trying to find his wife somewhere to sleep for the night. And Martin was the kind of man who offered help, not judgment.

Lolly tightened her hands into fists around the edge of the coverlet. He offered help when he saw the need for it. When he deemed the recipient to be on the wrong end of Society's judgment.

When she asked for that help, he scorned her. He had shut his eyes to her last night. Turned her away even though his member pulsed in her palm. Lolly didn't know much about bedroom activities, but she knew his body had been just as excited as hers.

And yet she had not been enough for him to throw off Societal expectations. Not even in private.

"I will put a stop to it," Papa said from the other room. "You have my word."

Lolly threw off her covers. Her nether regions were still a little wet, a little sensitive, from the way Martin had maneuvered them. Oh, for that glimpse of time, Lolly had felt so good. Blind, bound, captive to his fingers and tongue. She had lost all touch with intellect.

It only made his refusal that much worse.

She pushed off the thoughts. Her matters with Martin were secondary when Papa was currently putting a stop to Mr. and Mrs. Chow. Whatever that meant.

Since Northfield Hall hadn't been home to a lady for years, Lolly had been sharing her mother's personal abigail, Norton, while her sisters made do with one of the Preston housemaids. Norton rushed in at Lolly's call, a storm upon her face. "It's a bad start to the morning, I can tell you that, Lady Rosalind. Her ladyship woke up to see two foreigners among the household. It is enough to give a person a fright."

Lolly frowned at Norton's reflection in the mirror. "I don't see why my mother should feel surprise one way or another. It is not her household."

Norton tucked her chin and focused on pinning Lolly's hair.

"The fact of the matter is that Lord Preston hired Mr. and Mrs. Chow for their skills. Why, they were at Viscount Folkestone's household before this. It is a coup to have them at Northfield Hall instead."

"Begging your pardon, but they were let go from the viscount's household, so that is not a claim in their favor." Norton stuck a pin so that it scraped against Lolly's scalp. "My lady."

Lolly stood and held herself stiff as Norton settled the corset about her waist. "I thought you above gossip, Norton."

"It's not gossip if it is true. I'd say I heard it directly from them, except I doubt they can speak a word of English. Her ladyship has the right of it, Lady Rosalind, and you'd do well to follow her lead. Those people have no business being here. They are nothing but trouble."

She emphasized this with a pull so fierce that for a moment, Lolly thought she would never breathe again. Then the corset returned to its normal shape. Norton's rough hands reached around to tug her breasts upwards. They left white imprints on Lolly's skin.

Lolly tried not to compare it to how Martin had worshipped her breasts. She fixed her mind firmly on the image of poor, pregnant Mrs. Chow, nearly falling over in her husband's arms last night. Whatever happened next with Martin, Lolly's one goal must be to protect the Chows from her family.

It was a few more minutes as Norton piled on Lolly's petticoats, then her stomachier, and finally the yellow morning gown itself. All the while, Lolly turned words about in her mind, searching for the argument that would make Norton see. An appeal to sympathy would do nothing, she knew from experience. Neither would a simple rebuke, since Norton's loyalties lay with Mama. Finally, when Norton turned to leave, lips still pursed in disapproval, Lolly said, "That will be all, Norton. I must thank you for all your help this week. I'm sure it won't be necessary anymore, as Lord Preston hired Mrs. Chow as my maid."

Norton gaped. "She will burn you dead with the curling tongs!"

"I will thank you not to say such disparaging things of my fiance's household. You may go."

Lolly did not move so much as an eyebrow until Norton – still ashen with shock – backed out of the room. Straight to Mama, no doubt, to report that Lolly had been claimed by Satan.

Still, Lolly had won that exchange. In a small way, but not inconsequential.

No matter that she had no plans to actually marry Martin.

Louisa and Charlotte were the only ones in the breakfast room, bickering over whether it was proper to serve kedgeree on the same plate as toast. Lolly thought they didn't even notice her enter the room until Charlotte asked, "Do you know what has upset everyone this morning, Lolly?"

It was always a question how much to share with her sisters. On the one hand, Lolly liked an opportunity to gain them on her side. On the other, between the two of them, they could take an unpleasant topic the size of a thimble and talk into the size of a soup tureen.

She compromised on a vague answer. "Prejudice, Lotte, and perhaps a little pride."

Louisa rolled her eyes.

Lolly served a slice of spice cake onto a tea saucer. She was halfway towards the corridor when Louisa called, "You are sitting down, aren't you, Rosalind?"

As if she were their mother. Lolly didn't even turn around to reply, "I've simply too much to do. Ta!"

The household was indeed on edge. As Lolly crossed the front hall, Mr. Hewitt very nearly bowled her over, rushing to the back of the house so fast he didn't see her. Witnessing the incident, a parlor maid polishing the banister screamed as if a highwayman had stuck a gun to her back. And Mrs. Smollett emerged from the upper story to dress them down with a wicked tongue.

It filled Lolly's stomach with sour anger. Mr. and Mrs. Chow needed to be met with kindness, not with bedeviled chaos.

Suddenly without any appetite at all, Lolly set her plate on a side table and headed directly for Martin's study. Except instead of meeting her fiancé there, she found only Papa and poor Mr. Maulvi. She hung back in the threshold before they saw her.

"This is extremely out of the ordinary," Papa was lecturing Mr. Maulvi. He employed the quiet anger that always made Lolly quiver. "Seeing as you ran the household in Lord Preston's absence this last year, I fail to see why you cannot make this change now before he returns."

To his credit, Mr. Maulvi was not cowering away from Papa. "Lord Preston has only gone to Thatcham, my lord. He will return before luncheon."

"And he will not thank you for leaving this mess to him," Papa persisted. "Lord Preston should not be involved in the hiring of household servants in the first place. It is beneath him."

As Lolly saw it, she had two options: interrupt this argument and try to convince Papa he was wrong, or demonstrate better behavior for the rest of the household.

She wasn't brave enough for the first choice.

Backing away, Lolly cut through the rear drawing room into the garden, and from there to the outer building that housed the kitchen and pantry. She wasn't sure what the servants had done with the Chows, but she had a good feeling they weren't currently permitted in the Hall itself. Sure enough, as she pushed open the kitchen door, Lolly spotted none other than Mrs. Chow on her knees, scrubbing the stone floor.

"Oh, that won't do at all!" Lolly exclaimed before she could stop herself.

Cook, who had been leaning against the wooden countertop, straightened and curtsied. "Lady Rosalind."

It was clear as day that Cook – a tall woman in full health – had been watching the very pregnant woman rather than helping. Anger surged all the way to Lolly's tongue. "Is this the kind of household at Northfield Hall, then? Unfeeling and cruel? Really, it is plain to anyone with eyes that Mrs. Chow is not currently fit for such work. I cannot imagine what kind of Christian would put her to a task like this."

Cook went white, then red. Lolly really couldn't bring herself to care. Tapping Mrs. Chow on the shoulder – for she wasn't sure how much English the woman understood – Lolly helped her to her feet. Mrs. Chow's entire arms were trembling.

Lolly turned back to Cook. "Lord Preston hired Mrs. Chow as my personal lady's maid. She is not to be pressed into kitchen work again."

She only hoped Martin didn't mind her wielding his name behind false orders. Making sure Mrs. Chow followed, she marched out of the kitchen.

"I'm so sorry about that. It won't happen again. Are you feeling well?" Lolly turned to study Mrs. Chow's face for understanding. The other woman's eyes were watchful, but not confused.

"Yes, thank you, my lady." She spoke with an accent, as expected, and an unusual lilt to her sentences. As she continued, she did not always use the correct words, but Lolly pieced together her meaning. "I am not trained to be a lady's maid. I am better suited to the laundry, my lady."

"Not to worry. If you work in the laundry, then you know how to remove stains from my gowns, and the rest of it is gravy." Lolly smiled with this, but she saw exactly when Mrs. Chow stumbled over her phrasing. "I'll train you in the rest of it," she amended. "You will do splendidly."

She had been leading Mrs. Chow towards the grand staircase, intending to install the woman in her own apartment until Martin could give a final decree to the household. But as they entered the front hall, Lolly heard Papa stalking towards them from the study. From his footsteps alone, she could tell Mr. Maulvi had not capitulated, which meant Papa would be angrier than ever.

Lolly panicked.

Grabbing Mrs. Chow's hand, she rushed through the front door and then – when she heard Papa still approaching – into the hidden space between a giant azalea and the brick façade of Northfield Hall.

"I'm sorry," she whispered to Mrs. Chow as they both tried to crouch from sight. She thought the pregnant woman must be frightened out of her mind, but instead it looked like Mrs. Chow was trying to suppress a laugh.

"Even you have something to be frightened of," Mrs. Chow whispered back. "That makes us sisters."

Lolly grinned. "Yes, sisters."

They both sobered when Papa exited the house. He slammed the door behind him, as if that would teach Mr. Maulvi a lesson.

Or perhaps it wasn't Mr. Maulvi he was concerned about. Suddenly, Lolly heard a horse and vehicle coming down the drive. From her vantage point, squatting on the ground, she saw only Papa's boots and then – as the horse pulled the carriage around to the front of the house, hooves and slim wheels.

A cloud of dust drifted through the azalea directly under Lolly's nose.

"Lord Preston," Papa barked, "you have finally returned."

Martin's boots came into view now, older and dustier than Papa's. "I did not think you would feel my absence so keenly, my lord. I apologize. I had some small business to attend in Thatcham."

"I cannot imagine you left unaware of the great insult you have delivered to my family."

Lolly's nose twitched. She could feel the dust tickling her nostrils. She took a deep, silent breath, trying to ignore it.

"Insult?" Martin's joking tone had been replaced by bewilderment. "The last thing I would want to do is insult you, my lord."

"You hired two..." Papa's word was caught on the wind, but Lolly could feel it in her gut. She was glad not to hear it. "...without any references, to serve my family. It would be an insult to any gentleman, let alone your own betrothed. Worse, your man refused to listen to me and dismiss them in your stead. It is almost as if you ordered him to be obstinate to me."

Mrs. Chow began to tremble again. Slowly, Lolly repositioned so that the other woman could lean entirely against Lolly's back.

"I was not aware my father-in-law would involve himself in household affairs." There was an edge to Martin's voice now. "As for the Chows, I offered them positions as the Christian thing to do. They cannot return to their home parish. They are in need of assistance. I cannot see anything insulting about that."

Papa advanced forward a step. "Then let me help you see. You have not directed your man to enclose the fields. You have not written for the clover seeds from Macarius Abbey. You have not even committed to me your vote in the Hastings impeachment. You are a man of no action, except to hire criminals as servants for my daughter."

Even Mrs. Chow drew in her breath at this. Papa might as well have challenged Martin to a duel with such inflammatory language. Indeed, Martin's feet rearranged themselves into a solid, wide-legged stance, as if readying for a fight. "I am a man of actions with which you disagree, my lord, not a man of inaction. I will not apologize for living true to my honor."

"On the contrary, Lord Preston, you will apologize and send those criminals away before luncheon," Papa spat, "or you will not marry my daughter." And he stalked back into the house, slamming the door again behind him.

Lolly couldn't tell what Martin was thinking from the view of just his two feet. But her own heart leapt painfully from her chest. Papa didn't issue ultimatums like this on a whim. He wouldn't take it back.

He meant to stop her from marrying Martin. And even though Lolly burned at how Martin had turned her away, she hadn't decided yet what she wanted to do. There was a part of her that yearned for him to kiss her again. There was pure admiration, too. He didn't settle for reality. He didn't accept easy answers.

He was a nobleman in the truest sense of the word. And Lolly wasn't ready to refuse him, not even after the way he treated her last night.

She couldn't ask him to choose between herself and the Chows. She wouldn't. Lolly would go to Boston, and Mr. and Mrs. Chow could have their baby safely at Northfield Hall.

It only took her one moment to resolve her mind. To be at peace with it.

And then the next moment came. Mrs. Chow shifted suddenly, putting more weight than ever on Lolly. At the same time, the breeze threw grit directly at Lolly's face. And there was nothing she could do to stop it.

Lolly sneezed.

At first, Martin's heart was hammering too fast to register the sound. He couldn't tear his eyes from the door. It looked so peaceful now that it had closed behind Turner. It didn't look like the sole barrier between himself and disaster.

And then his ears caught up with the rest of his brain. That had been no dainty sneeze. It had torn through its emitter like a hurricane through an armada, wreaking mucus in its wake. There was only one woman to whom it could belong.

He looked over his shoulder, expecting to find Lolly turning the corner of the house from the garden path. But there was no one.

Then came another sneeze, just as forceful as the last, and the azalea bush quaked. Martin spotted a yellow gown, then the brown puff of her hair.

"Are you hiding?" he asked as a strange spasm of emotion seized him. It started at a dizzying mix of delight and desire but dissolved into something else. Shame. Frustration. Sorrow.

With much rustling, Lolly stood. Mrs. Chow rose, too, looking pale.

Guilt slammed Martin's chest.

"We didn't want Papa to find us." Lolly stepped onto the drive, as natural as if she were emerging from a drawing room, then extended a hand to help Mrs. Chow do the same. "I decided Mrs. Chow should train as my lady's maid. Obviously, that is only what we will say until I leave, but you must find something else for her that does not involve scrubbing floors. She shouldn't be working hard at all in her condition."

Lolly did not meet his eyes as she said this. He guessed it was because she so neatly skirted the issue of eavesdropping. But a part of him – an ugly, desperate part of him – wanted it to be because she had changed her mind, that she actually did want to marry him.

He knew it couldn't be that. Not after last night. He hadn't gotten any sleep, had only twisted himself in his sheets puzzling out the moral question she had posed. He was willing to concede that on principle, a woman had the right to experience extramarital intercourse just as much as a man. If she was well aware of the potential consequences of the affair, then Martin would allow that she should therefore have the right to do with her body what she would. Lolly, therefore, had done no wrong in propositioning him last night.

That did not give her the right to force him. To shame him for wanting to think it through. To reject him merely because he wanted to protect her honor. Martin could still feel her hands yanking his cock, as if she deserved to do whatever she wanted with it simply because she had the right to proposition him.

At dawn, Martin concluded two things: he had done well to stand his ground, and he had no hope of winning Lolly's hand after doing so.

Martin would let her go gracefully. He had ridden to Thatcham that morning specifically to post her letter to Frances so that she would be welcomed in Boston when she chose to leave. Now Turner had further removed all hope of matrimony between them. Martin had gone dizzy from having Lolly in his life; from here, he could only cherish the memory of her taste as he wished her well.

It was the right thing to do.

Clearing his throat, he responded to her comments. "Yes, of course. I instructed Mrs. Smollett to let Mrs. Chow rest today to recover from her journey, in any case." To Mrs. Chow, he added, "You must not let them bully you."

"What did you do at home, before you came to England?" Lolly asked. "Silk weaving, perhaps?"

Mrs. Chow laughed as if Lolly had suggested something as ridiculous as growing tobacco. In broken English, she said, "No, my lady. My father was the village butcher."

She had been raised to run her own home, then. Better suited as a housekeeper or nurse than a common servant, but Martin was in need of neither.

"A parlor maid, perhaps," Lolly said. She looked down, shaking her skirts of azalea blossoms and twigs. "No fear, Mrs. Chow, Lord Preston will sort it out. I am only sorry I won't be able to get to know you better as my maid."

Mrs. Chow looked from Lolly to Martin and back again, a frown slowly creasing her brow. "I do not understand. Are my lord and lady no longer getting married?"

Martin couldn't help but run his eyes over Lolly. Beautiful and proud, just like the first morning he had proposed to her. And now he knew how she felt in his arms, the heat of her skin and the complexity of her scent and the tremor in her breath when he kissed her. The way her thighs molded to him like ivy to a tree.

He jerked his gaze upward and found her watching him just as intently.

She had never been his. He understood that now. The engagement had been misguided all along. She was meant for something more than being the delight of his life.

And he couldn't do the wrong thing. Not even for her.

"No, we are not," he answered Mrs. Chow.

Chapter Ten

It wasn't until Martin rejected her that Lolly knew what she wanted. And when she knew, she knew – from the deepest marrow of her bones to the screaming tears behind her eyes.

She wanted to marry him.

She wanted to spend the rest of her days kissing him and debating with him. She wanted to be in his arms; she wanted to watch him eat his favorite meals; she wanted to pick her way through her life with him in search of the best way to do right. At Frances's orphanage, Lolly may have been able to help forgotten children and instill them with a sense of goodness, but with Martin, she could forge her own way. They could turn Northfield Hall into an orphanage, or move to London to crusade for better poor relief, or give up all their worldly belongings and join a lecture circuit around the countryside.

He was a good man. A handsome man. A kind man. And she wanted him to be hers.

"Actually, we are," Lolly declared. Martin stared at her, his cheeks going pale. Pale because of shock, or because he didn't want to marry her anymore? "I'm sorry for how I behaved last night. I shouldn't have been so forceful, and I shouldn't have left. We still need to argue it out. I want to fix it. I want to be your wife."

Martin's gaze flicked towards Mrs. Chow. "Perhaps you did not hear Lord Turner..."

"My father can say whatever he wants. I am of age. I may do what I please. And it pleases me to marry you."

Now Martin's face transformed again. His eyes shimmered. His mouth softened. His whole body lilted, as if on the breeze, towards her.

Mrs. Chow beamed at them. "Give him a kiss, my lady!"

They were in full view of anyone who looked out the window, but Lolly didn't care. She stepped into Martin's embrace, wrapping his hands about her waist and nestling her face to his. His lips met hers chastely at first, and then the taste of his tongue raced into her bloodstream.

"I'm not going to be an easy wife," she said between kisses. "I will say no to things, sometimes without knowing why." She bit at his lower lip. "I will insist our daughters have the same education as our sons." She got distracted by his tongue again. "I will be headstrong and obstinate and all the other things a lady is not supposed to be."

"Don't forget your sneezing," Martin said, drifting his lips to her earlobe. "You will sneeze like a blacksmith whenever you want, no matter how importune. Even during our relations."

"Especially during relations." Lolly pressed her palms to his shoulders to hold herself away. He was so handsome, this man who had helped her on the balcony without even showing her his face. She didn't know how she had gotten so lucky. "Will you still have me, even despite all that?"

"No." Martin's gaze was so somber, so earnest, that rejection stung Lolly, and she drew back. But his hands held her in place against him. "I will marry you because of all that."

This time, they didn't kiss. They wrapped their arms around each other and clung. Lolly tried to think what it felt like, to be held so tight and fast, but she didn't know of anything at all similar. She was safe. She was cherished. She was his.

"Now, how would you like to handle this?" Martin asked into her ear. "Shall I ride to Lambeth Palace to purchase a special license?"

That would be the easiest way. He could steal her away from the London townhouse at the break of dawn for a quiet wedding, so that her parents couldn't stop them.

But Lolly knew the difference between easy and right.

"No." Slowly, reluctantly, she peeled away from him. "I will go speak to my father."

Northfield Hall was bustling when they reentered. The parlor maid who had been polishing the banister had left, replaced by two maids and a footman hurrying upstairs with valises. Footsteps paced the ceiling above, and Mama's shrill voice drifted down with muffled directions to Norton.

Papa had meant it, then. He was removing them from Northfield entirely. All because Martin dared show charity to two lost immigrants.

Anger surged through her anew.

Lolly led Mrs. Chow to her apartment first and settled her on the settee beside the window. Then, closing the door firmly behind her, Lolly headed to her parents' suite.

If she hadn't known the context, she might have thought the scene she encountered a tableau of quiet domesticity. Papa sat at the center table, legs stretched as if to take up the whole room. Louisa hovered behind him, pouring dark coffee from a silver carafe. Opposite, Mama stood in her lace-trimmed dressing robe, casting directions to Norton. And Charlotte perched on a stool, examining the hem of her skirt.

There was no place for Lolly in the family scene. Nor did she want there to be. Not when it was predicated by her parents' uncontrollable fear.

"Papa, I must speak with you."

Even though impatience steeled his every feature, his face softened when he looked at her. "There you are." Rising, Papa wrapped both her hands in his. The grasp was unpleasantly warm. "I'm afraid there has been a distressing change of plans. We have been disappointed, Lolly. Lord Preston is not the gentleman I believed him to be. We return to London at once."

Papa was always the one to break bad news to her. When her favorite doll disappeared into the harbor. When her nursemaid refused to quit Boston with them. When Ned offered marriage to Ursula instead of her.

He knew just how to mold his voice into something soft and comforting. How to tilt his lips into a promise that the world would eventually right itself. How to offer love through nothing more than his touch.

But this time, all Lolly saw was his effort. She watched him draw on every skill, as if she were a puppet whose strings he could control. It wasn't comfort he offered her, not this time. This was manipulation.

Pure and simple.

Lolly removed her hands from his grip. "I am marrying Lord Preston."

"We will find you someone else," Papa continued, as if she hadn't spoken. "Someone worthy of the Turner family. It will work out better than ever. You'll see."

"I am marrying Lord Preston," she repeated. Her voice caught on her fear and tripped out of her mouth. But she said it. "With or without your permission."

Papa stared at her. For a moment, his frown was sympathetic. Then it grew darker. "He has offended our family, and he refuses to acknowledge his behavior. I know this is a disappointment, Lolly, but you must trust that I am doing what is right."

This was difficult. Worse than she had expected. Her palms were sweating; her fingers trembling.

She had never refused Papa before.

"Our family has no right to be offended. Lord Preston did the Christian thing in offering work to a couple far from their home parish. Their presence is not insulting. In any case, he asked me before hiring them. Last night in the garden."

Now Mama fluttered over. "Do not contradict your father, Rosalind."

Papa drew his hands behind his back, which he always did when he decided a conversation was at its end. Fear slithered through Lolly; she could suddenly feel how much smaller she was compared to her father.

Not that he would ever hurt her.

"You do not see the situation clearly," he said in a tone that brooked no argument. "You are clouded by your tendre for Lord Preston. I do not fault you for it, but I must insist you pack your things. Once this is all behind you, you will understand why."

A week ago, Lolly would never have disobeyed her father when he used such a tone. Even had he decreed they must leave London for St. Petersburg and never return. Even had he ordered her to chop off her own left hand.

That was when she had believed her father tried his best to do the right thing.

She knew better now.

"I already understand why, Papa. Your world needs order. You cannot stand when that order is upturned. You are lashing out because you are frightened of what will happen if you let kindness seep in."

His face turned bright red. Lolly kept speaking before he could interrupt her.

"I am not afraid of that. I am afraid of what will happen if we are so protective of order that we stop helping those who need it. The truth is –" She hadn't planned on saying this, of all things. But suddenly, she needed to confess it, or it would burn through her life. "– Lord Preston and I planned to end this engagement in a few months, once the scandal had blown over. I didn't want to marry a stranger simply because he helped rescue my skirts from a balcony. We decided to say we were engaged so people wouldn't talk. But then I learned what kind of man he is. Kind. Considerate. And brave – so brave, Papa. He isn't afraid of losing anyone's good opinion or power or anything, not so long as he does the right thing by the people who depend upon him. He is not concerned about keeping order. He is concerned about making sure every man can feed his own family."

Papa's mouth was flapping, as if to speak, and Lolly was almost out of words. But not quite.

"I love him, Papa. I want the life he offers me. One that is dedicated to people besides myself. Or my family. You can't talk me out of this. You can't stop me. I will marry Lord Preston, with or without your permission."

The room was silent for a moment. Everyone stared at her. Lolly was hot and out of breath. She had never spoken her feelings so clearly or loudly before. It was an exhausting enterprise.

Then Charlotte squealed, "Oh, but it is so romantic!"

"It's not romantic, it's foolish!" Louisa hushed as Mama turned to them with a scold, "Off to your packing, the both of you."

Papa squared his shoulders. He was no longer red, no longer sputtering. He was pale and so very in control. "If you marry against my wishes, the consequences are clear. You will no longer receive your dowry. You will no longer visit our family. You will no longer be my daughter."

Lolly had heard of this type of punishment. When a daughter ran off with the footman, or if she paraded herself naked through the streets. She had imagined her father might strike her off the family tree when she fled to Boston.

But never for marrying the man he had forced her to accept in the first place.

It hurt in a physical way, squeezing her heart and stomach and lungs into a vise. Yet it did not change her mind. The tableau had changed – Louisa and Charlotte now being ushered out by Norton, Mama holding smelling salts to her nose, and Papa waiting steely-eyed for her response – but it was still the aristocratic family protecting itself.

Without examining what it protected itself from.

Lolly stepped back from her parents. "Disown me if you so choose. You must make your decisions, and I must make mine."

"Lolly, you don't mean that," Mama cried. Papa wrapped his arm around Mama's shoulders. For the first time, he looked old. Frail.

She couldn't regret this. Couldn't regret choosing Martin and the Chows and all that was good over her family.

But Lolly wished it didn't have to be this way.

"I love you," she said, "no matter what."

And then she walked away.

MARTIN HEARD IT ALL. He had tried not to; Lolly had clearly wanted to speak to her father alone, so he had turned towards his own rooms to change out of his riding clothes. But their voices had carried, arresting him on the landing.

Now Lolly came flying down the hall, pale as death. She didn't see him, nor did she seem to have a destination. She only fled.

I love him, she had said. At the price of her family.

He caught her into his arms as she passed him. She fought him off at first, until her eyes focused and she realized it was him. Then she froze, taut as a violin string. "I won't have a dowry."

Martin didn't care. "I love you too."

"They won't speak to us again."

"You'll change their minds." He rearranged his arms, pulling her closer against him, and finally Lolly relaxed a little. Her palms rested on his chest. "You had to have inherited your stubbornness from somewhere, after all."

In the guest suite, there was a crash of furniture falling, followed by a curse that would make a sailor blush. Lolly closed her eyes. "What if they never forgive me?"

Martin wanted to promise her that it would all resolve itself. He wanted to offer to fix it himself, or guarantee that his love would be enough to replace her family. His heart was so full from her declaration that he felt as if he could change the world, starting with Turner's cruelty and ending with every imbalance in the economy.

He curtailed the impulse. "Will you forgive me for making you choose?"

She shook her head. "You didn't make me choose."

"If I turn the Chows out now, your father would make peace with us." He held his breath, knowing he couldn't do it.

"That would be the worst thing."

"Still, by not doing so, I am making you choose between your family and me."

Lolly's eyes fanned open now, and she looked fierce again. "Papa is making us choose, and we are choosing the same thing."

"So then, the question is: what if you never forgive him?"

Tears welled suddenly in her eyes, and one spilled onto her cheek. Martin watched it fall. Better to hold her steady than to stop her from weeping.

"I love you too, Lolly," he said again because he wasn't sure she had heard him the first time. "I will love you for the rest of my life, whether we are together or apart. I can't wait to marry you, and I will do everything in my power to stop anyone from hurting you like this again. But the more we try to do things differently, the more people will turn us away. It is worth it to me. I love that it is worth it to you, too. When we have children, it will be worth it to them. That is all I can offer you. I hope it is enough."

She kissed him. It was good she did, because he had begun to talk himself into a reality where she refused him in favor of an easier life. He tasted her tears – there were more of them now – but other than that, the kiss was giving. Comforting. Like they had been kissing for decades already, instead of just the one day.

The corridor exploded with commotion as the Turners expelled from their suite. Martin tugged Lolly away from the stairs, but he didn't let her go. Her family marched in their traveling clothes. Lord Turner glared; Lady Turner didn't look at them at all. Louisa raised a haughty eyebrow at Lolly before sweeping down the stairs. Only Charlotte broke rank, throwing her arms about both of them. "I wish you every happiness. Write to me," she whispered.

Then she scampered after the family out to the awaiting carriage.

Lolly leaned against Martin. The servants still had much to do before the family could depart; it would be hours before the commotion was truly over. He had to check on Mr. Chow, too, and sit down with Mr. Maulvi for the regular day's work.

But Lolly was soft and warm and heavy beside him. They had slayed a dragon together, and this was their sunset. "All in all," he said, a smile on his lips, "I'm glad it was you sneezing on that balcony."

Lolly laughed. "What luck that Lady Leighster screamed it for everyone to hear."

"She should try her hand at matchmaking. I am in her debt for the rest of time."

They grinned at each other. Then, with a last peck to his lips, Lolly pushed away. "No use dawdling. I must see to Mrs. Chow." She threw him a look over her shoulder. "Fair warning: I mean to try again tonight. I expect you to have finished your philosophizing by the time I arrive."

Martin's cock leaped to attention.

He already knew how he would respond.

Epilogue

THE LILACS BLOOMED IN time for the birthday party. Lolly sat back against the old oak tree to admire them. The first few years after she planted them, they hadn't blossomed at all, and she thought she must have killed them. But now the trees were perfectly pear-shaped, the purple and white flowers bowing beautifully to the breeze.

Benjamin lunged at her suddenly, thrusting little Caroline into her arms. "Mama, she smells again."

Indeed she did, stinking of a toddler mess. Lolly took her carefully so that Caro only touched her apron. "Thank you, Benny, I'll see to it."

He dashed back to the pond. Martin had decreed that everyone except Caro could swim today, since the afternoon was warm and he was there to save Nate if the seven-year-old faltered in the water. Ellen and Sophia, inseparable as always even in their adolescence, were already racing each other from one edge to the other. Benjamin stripped to his underclothes with the unleashed enthusiasm of a ten-year-old and jumped in. The girls shrieked at the splash; Nate lashed his arms about Benny's neck as if to drown him; and Martin shook his head from his perch on the grass, his hair and jacket and trousers now splattered with pond water.

He joined her under the oak trees as Lolly turned her attention to changing Caroline's linens. They had given Nurse a whole week off in the good weather to visit her family, and Lolly didn't mind getting hands-on with her daughter in the meantime.

"Do you think she is enjoying her party?" Martin asked, pulling a silly face at Caro.

"She hasn't the faintest idea what is happening except that everyone else is having fun." After wiping the baby clean, Lolly pressed a kiss onto her stomach. Caro giggled. She was the happiest two-year-old in the world, so long as she had someone smiling at her. As soon as Lolly finished changing her, Caro would take off racing unsteadily around the picnic blanket with pure joy. "Two already. Can you believe it?"

She was their last baby; the doctor had made that clear. Lolly couldn't complain, not with five children leaping about her, and her body certainly appreciated a rest after over a decade of mothering. Still, Lolly loved having a baby about. She would miss the soft skin and coos and simple demands when Caroline joined her siblings in scapering about the estate.

"I can no more believe it than I can that we have been married for fifteen years." Martin slid his arm around Lolly. He smelled as he always did: like the center of her universe. She leaned in so that he could dot a kiss or two along her head.

Fifteen years since he had first shown her this pond. Fifteen years since her father had last spoken to her.

"Any regrets?" Martin asked, as if he could hear her thoughts.

"None." Smiling, Lolly handed him the dirty clout. The linen, just like the rest of their summer clothes, were made from the flax grown right here in the Northfield common fields. Old Man Swann – once a sailor in the King's navy – raised sheep in the southern pastures for woolen goods. The food they ate, the soap and candles they consumed, the carriages they rode, everything was grown or manufactured within fifty miles of Northfield. Martin had funded the start of any industry they needed, taking particular care to invest in people who needed help the most. Displaced colonialists, like the Chows, and people escaped from slave territories. Unwed mothers who had been turned away from their families. Sailors and soldiers who couldn't find income after serving the Crown.

Northfield was more than Lolly could have imagined that day when she chose Martin over her family. They had found a way to grow a community out of misfits and orphans. London had not been very kind to them, but Lolly didn't need the approval of Society matrons. She spent her days teaching at the village school, writing articles for forward-thinking lady's magazines, and stealing moments with her children. Every day, she found hope and inspiration and joy in the life she and Martin had created.

They were lucky. Fifteen years of marriage, fifteen years of health, fifteen years of spiritual wealth. If Lolly died tomorrow, she would die happy.

"Here come Mr. Maulvi and Mrs. Croft with the cake," Martin said as Lolly tied up Caroline's clothes.

"Is that the Chows behind them?" The tradition was to give everyone the day off on a birthday. Lolly always expected the household to scatter to their own families, yet every time, the celebration turned into a huge party with most of the estate turning out.

One day, she would learn to plan for it.

In the meantime, she turned to Martin for a final kiss. He lingered, nipping at her lower lip. If they had truly been alone, they would have lost the next half hour in each other. As it was, Lolly teased his tongue until Ellen yelled from the pond, "Stop kissing!"

"Indeed," Mr. Maulvi said, placing the cake on the picnic blanket spread beneath the oak trees. "Think what kind of example you are setting." And he promptly caught Mrs. Croft in a similar embrace, earning a chorus of groans from the children.

Then Mr. and Mrs. Chow arrived with their three youngest offspring, and Mr. Chow dipped Mrs. Chow into the most scandalous kiss of all.

The wind picked up, stirring enough pollen from the lilacs that Lolly and each one of her children let out a loud sneeze. Martin grinned even as he had to marshal extra handkerchiefs from the picnic basket. Then everyone settled, sitting criss-cross or lying on their stomachs or leaning against their spouse. Lolly sliced the cake while

Mr. Maulvi started spinning an adventure tale. With the children captive and Caro eating cake messily in her lap, Lolly murmured to Martin, "It is a perfect day."

"Just one of many," he replied, and it was true. Lolly was the luckiest woman in England.

She resolved to enjoy it for as long as she could.

Author's Note

THE ROMANCE GENRE IS all about fantasy. At its core, there is the fantasy of true love that cannot be broken by circumstance or time or evil. On top of that, each subgenre has its own trimmings, like wearing the most beautiful gown at a ball, moving into a house with the perfect library, and of course, intense sex that is always satisfying.

I wrote this novella to create my own little fantasy: heroes and heroines in Regency England who had economic power but who didn't profit from slavery and imperialism. You see, the more I researched little details for my previous books (like, what kind of fabric would a dress be made of? Would sugar be available? How would this family have earned their wealth?) the more I discovered that the rich, noble characters we love to read about in Regency romances are all dependent upon slavery and the subjugation of native peoples and economies throughout the world.

Setting up a new ecosystem at Northfield Hall is my way of divorcing the fantasy of the rich and titled world from that reality. It started as a thought exercise – what if I created a family that didn't profit off slave or subjugated labor? – and turned into this story. In this novella, I had to figure out why Martin and Lolly would choose to separate themselves from the economics of the day and how that would shape their relationship. There are a lot of elements in setting up a household that boycotts basically all imports that I am probably oversimplifying or not considering or simply basing on a bad theory. But this is not an economics textbook. It is my fantasy.

As always, I have some people to thank for helping bring The Baron without Blame to life. Julia Gerbach designs my beautiful covers while Sara Israel serves as my stalwart proofreader on this project. Thank you to my beta readers: Sarah Flanagan (PhD), Jen Trinh, Jules O'Dowd, and Sarah Hopgood. Also, thank you my husband, who gives me feedback, encouragement, and is the inspiration behind sexy sneezes. (But let's add tissues to the grocery list, okay?) Finally, thank you to my family, friends, and all of you for wanting to read what is next!

The Countess Without Conviction

Katherine Grant

What to Expect from The Countess Without Conviction

IS THEIR MARRIAGE STRONG ENOUGH TO WEATHER THIS STORM?

Ever since their wedding day, Ellen Preston and Max Hainsworth have happily ignored the fact that one day they would become the Earl and Countess Meretta. **When Max inherits his title, their life is upended - and a storm begins to brew.**

Returning from a long parliamentary season in London, **Max discovers that things are not going well for Ellen at their**

new home of Montchampion Manor. His mother is critical of the new countess, the carpenters don't want Ellen in the workshop, and everyone is upset that Ellen and Max want to ban imports of tea and cotton.

Worst of all, Ellen seems to have lost her faith in Max.

Ellen is doing her best to adjust to her new life, but the house is too big, the servants are too suspicious, and Max is too distant. **When nasty rumors make her question everything she believes in, she and Max must find a way to unite again - or risk forever being torn apart.**

YOU'LL ENJOY THIS STORY IF YOU HAVE PREVIOUSLY READ THE VISCOUNT WITHOUT VIRTUE. HAPPILY-EVER-AFTER GUARANTEED!

For content advisories, please visit www.katherinegrantromance.com/contentadvisories.

The Reunion

From the sitting room of Montchampion Manor, Ellen could not see Max.

More properly said, from the blue-wallpapered room designated as the family's sitting room—only for use when there was absolutely no company expected!—Ellen could see the last quarter mile of the curved drive up to the manor, but Max was not to be seen.

Which did not mean he was not currently on the drive. Even had she been in the front sitting room with its gilded ceiling and expansive windows, she would not have been able to see *more* than the last curve of the drive, since the entire five-mile stretch had been designed to keep visitors from glimpsing the great house until its very last leg, when the trees cleared and one had a direct prospect of the marble monstrosity waiting to intimidate.

And while Max might not be on the last curve of the drive, that did not mean that he was not at this very moment somewhere along its five miles, galloping forward at full speed to finally return to his family.

In any case, the dowager countess would not hear of them waiting for Max in any room except the blue sitting room. She disapproved of the way Ellen stood with her forehead nearly pressed against the window, but though Ellen could feel and absorb that disapproval, she did not have to change her behavior just because Lady Odette willed it, and so she remained, looking out the window for signs of her husband.

Rosalind, Ellen's eight-year-old, sat with great composure on the sofa with Lady Odette. "We must be ladylike as we wait, Mama," she admonished Ellen, repeating the dictate her grandmother had given when the note arrived two hours ago announcing that Max was to be expected that afternoon.

"The earl will not get here any sooner if we smear the windows with our anticipation," Lady Odette added, her words a little thick with her French accent.

Even after nearly a year, Ellen was not accustomed to Max being the earl. The Earl of Meretta. Which made her the Countess of Meretta. Those titles belonged to other people, in Ellen's mind; the earl had always been a political adversary to Papa, and even after she married Max, she had cringed if she heard the appellation.

Now when people said *the Earl of Meretta*, they meant Max. Charming, arrogant, thoughtful, infuriating, wonderful Max. And Ellen got caught between her instinctual cringe and the comforting embrace of love that came with thinking of her husband.

Lady Odette poured peppermint tea into her cup with precision, allowing the tisane to tinkle against the delicate imported Chinese porcelain. "I daresay the wait *would* be easier if we had tea."

The wait would be easier if they didn't have to do it together. Ellen would have been perfectly happy to greet Max on her own, or to gather up their five children and walk out to meet him, or to busy her hands with some task instead of watching the road. Yet Lady Odette had *insisted* that there was a proper way to do this. Banish the four younger children to the nursery—"One does not want to overwhelm the poor man with their youthful cries the very minute he walks in!"—assemble in the blue room—"He will be famished and thirsty and need refreshments immediately"—and wait in near stillness—"What better way to greet the earl than by presenting a perfect tableau?"

And since Ellen *had* eradicated tea and coffee from Montchampion Manor—along with other imports like sugar, cotton, rice, and tobacco—she was trying to accommodate her mother-in-law with these requests to be "ladylike."

It would be easier if Lady Odette would just move into the dower house and live her own life.

Suddenly, Max appeared on the drive. He rode his gray stallion (named Shortcake by Rosalind four years ago) and moved in a canter that he made look as natural as walking. His blond hair peeked out from under his hat, his white skin a little tanner than she remembered, his arms and legs looking just as muscular as they had when he left.

Ellen had to curl her fingers into fists to keep herself from racing from the room to meet him outside.

She hadn't seen him for four months. He had been in London, where, as a member of the House of Lords, he had been required to attend the trial of Queen Caroline or be fined hundreds of pounds. And Ellen had been here, trying to convert Montchampion Manor from the seat of an egotistical aristocrat to another Northfield Hall.

They were accustomed to being apart for parliamentary seasons. Ellen hated London, but she and Max both wanted him there, first as an elected MP in the House of Commons and now, as an earl, in his birthright seat in the House of Lords.

The difference was that in years prior, Ellen had always been left behind at Northfield Hall. Her family's home, where she knew and trusted just about everyone she came across. Where she had a place in the carpentry workshop whenever she could make it there. Where the whole community tried to live by its best morals by avoiding imports and sharing the profits of the estate.

She always missed Max when he was gone. She had never before *needed* him so desperately.

It was shocking how angry she was at him for leaving her.

Because they were waiting for him in the blue room instead of rushing out to meet him, it was another eternity after Ellen sighted him before Max finally entered. His hat, gloves, and traveling coat had disappeared. He spotted Rosalind first and gathered her up in his arms, swinging her through the air. "You've gotten at least a foot taller!"

Lady Odette extended her hand from where she sat on the sofa. "Welcome back, Meretta."

When he had been viscount—the mere heir to the earldom—his parents had called him by his courtesy title, Berwick. Now, his name had changed, but still his mother refused to use the Christian name she herself had given him.

Max bowed in front of her dutifully and kissed her hand. "Are you well, Mother?"

"Well enough." She held onto his hand and murmured something in French, too soft and low for Ellen to hear.

Ellen knew she should not feel neglected. A heart had space for a daughter, a mother, *and* a wife.

It was just that the room felt so crowded, and Max hadn't yet greeted her.

She moved from the window. Rosalind, glowing with excitement at Max's arrival, rushed to her side. At last, Max was turning away from his mother. He was looking over his shoulder, and soon his gaze would land on her.

Ellen opened her mouth to say the perfect thing. Yet when finally she was looking directly into his hazel eyes, all that came out was, "I trust it did not rain while you were traveling."

He blinked in surprise. He bowed at the neck, a formal gesture he would offer a stranger. "Thank you, it did not."

For a moment, they stared at each other. Max did not approve of kissing in front of his mother, yet Ellen waited, wondering if she could hold out her arms and receive a hug. They hadn't seen each other for four months. They hadn't held each other for four months. And Ellen knew Max was a physical man; when they had first met, he couldn't keep his hands off her even though he should have.

Surely he was yearning for touch as much as she was.

Unless, as Lady Odette kept hinting, he had a mistress in London making sure he had all the touches he required.

Rosalind squirmed out from where Ellen gripped her two shoulders. "Do you want to see my paintings? Grandmama says my watercolors are very good. They are in the nursery. Grandmama says you don't want to go there. May I fetch them and bring them down?"

Max took his daughter's outstretched hand. "I should love to see them, but only if you take me up to them in the nursery. Is that where you have hidden your brothers and sisters, too?"

"Oh yes, only *I* didn't hide them. Grandmama said you weren't to be disturbed by their wailing the very first minute you came home."

"Ah, well, Grandmama doesn't realize how much I have missed their wailing." The two were already halfway into the corridor. Max paused, looking over his shoulder at Ellen again. The good humor he had offered Rosalind seemed to disappear as he asked, "Aren't you coming, too, Mama?"

Ellen didn't know why she said no, but she did.

Someone—Ellen? Mother?—had determined they would celebrate his homecoming with an elegant supper, and so Max ignored his better instincts and reported to the red sitting room in his formal black evening jacket.

His mother had beaten him there. She wore an extravagant silk gown adorned with gold braid that matched the gilded-framed paintings on the wall. As usual, her silver hair towered above her head, and a heavy necklace of dark sapphires sparkled on her neck.

"You look just like Meretta," she said as he bent to kiss her hand. "Your father, I mean."

Max tried to hide his grimace. His relationship with his father had been complicated for most of his life and then, for the last nine years, it had been nonexistent. He had chosen to marry Ellen, daughter of the earl's political enemy, and live the questionable lifestyle of Northfield Hall, where only British goods were consumed and all the estate's profits were shared by every single person who lived and worked there.

He had no choice in assuming his father's place as Earl of Meretta. That was predestined by British law, avoidable only by death.

But if he could help it, Max wouldn't be like his father in any other way, shape, or form.

Her eyes adjusting to something behind him, Mother added, "Is he not very handsome, my dear?"

Max turned. Ellen stood close to the door, as if she were already considering making a run for it. She had changed into her version of an evening gown. It was elegant in its simplicity: perfectly tailored dark blue wool with lace trim to define the shape of the bodice. Max knew this gown well, had seen her wear it a hundred times, had missed it while he was in London.

His mother said, "Meretta, you must buy your wife more jewels. She refuses to wear mine, and without them, anyone could mistake her for a governess."

Ellen's cheeks flushed. Max opened his mouth to defend her, but she beat him to it: "There is no one here to mistake me, unless you think *Meretta* has forgotten who I am in his long absence."

Her venom surprised Max. His wife was not a person who wielded words as weapons. She was earnest to a fault; even when Max himself had insulted her family when they first met, she had never returned the vitriol.

Neither did she use his title, unless they were in formal company. Even then, she was more likely to say "my husband." They had never discussed it, yet Max had always known that she did it purposefully, since he had chafed for so long at being defined by his title instead of as a person in his own right.

He didn't like how she wielded it now. Worse was how she didn't even look at Max as she threw out this rebuttal. She drifted instead to a different corner of the room, almost as far from Max and his mother as she could get, and put all her attention on the painting of a joyful family and their faithful servant.

Max knew Ellen was unhappy at Montchampion Manor. Their reunion had been awkward enough to hint that things had only gotten worse in his absence.

Now Max feared it was *him* she was upset with, and not the circumstances.

"You are unforgettable," he said in reply to her barb, "and the gown needs no adornment when it is worn by a beauty."

Ellen didn't turn from the painting. Of course not. She didn't like manufactured compliments traded in drawing rooms. Max wished he had ended his sentence with "unforgettable."

From her seat, Mother chimed in, "Well said, Meretta. Surely you feel lucky, Ellen, that your husband is so charming."

Which made Max want to expel his mother from the room entirely. What he needed was a moment—or an hour—alone with Ellen to sort out what was going on.

Mother would not stand for such things, not when the china was already laid for supper.

Still, he could say *something* to save both him and Ellen from being forced into false agreement. He put his hand on his mother's to quiet her, and was about to come up with the perfect response when the butler—who was new and whose name Max did not yet know—announced supper was ready.

"Excellent." Mother rose and tucked her hand into Max's elbow. "You will lead me in, Meretta. A mother misses her son when he is gone for so long."

As did a wife. But Max found himself without an option. He looked back over his shoulder to see how Ellen responded.

She still stood by that painting, her gaze fixed on something small and faraway.

Ellen told herself to buck up. Max was home at last. He had not remained in London longer than necessary—as she had begun to fear he might—and he would put things to rights for her. There was no reason to snipe at him, especially when it was Lady Odette who was being awful to begin with.

She would walk into the dining room with a new attitude. One that reflected the joy and gratitude she knew were frolicking around in her heart somewhere.

Let Lady Odette call her a governess. Let her whole meal revolve around preserving Lady Odette's fragile sense of world order. Ellen would bear it all, for at last Max was home.

Her seat was to the right of Max, with Lady Odette opposite her on his left. The rest of the polished mahogany table stretched down the room, its chairs perfectly placed in case another dozen guests arrived to join them. Ellen pretended she was on show for all the Londoners Max had just left behind. She smiled, she simpered, and she even accepted a glass of the French wine Lady Odette had insisted they serve.

"I have letters for you," Max told her as the footmen switched the fish for a collection of roasted meats. He leaned close; underneath the table, his leg brushed against the folds of her skirts, which in turn teased her bare knee.

It was almost as if they had touched.

"A fat one from your father, a funny one from Sophia, and one each from Nate and Caro that I couldn't judge from their appearance alone."

"You needn't judge the letters one way or another." He was teasing, so she tried to tease back. "They are to me, not you, after all."

"Ah, but I have long since worried that your correspondents are trying to whisk you away from me." Max winked, a smirk on his lips, and Ellen almost felt normal again. He was referring to that moment before they were married when she had received a letter thinking it was from him, yet in fact it was from a different man declaring his intentions to make her his bride.

Lady Odette interrupted: "Tell me more of London, Meretta. Did you see any theater?"

Max returned to the center of his seat. "Oh yes. There was a terrific opera. *Orfeo*. It follows the myth of Orpheus and Eurydice. Are you familiar with it?"

This he asked Ellen. There was a startling intensity to his eyes as they met hers, as if a great deal depended upon her answering yes. She could only reply honestly: "I don't remember it well."

"Orpheus and Eurydice are lovers, but Eurydice is killed by a snakebite. Orpheus makes a deal with Hades to revive her. If he can lead her out of Hades without looking back to see that she is behind him, then they can both live. If he looks back—even once—then Eurydice will die forever."

Ellen remembered it ended in tragedy, the same as the other Greek myths. Still, Max was looking at her as if he wanted her to ask. There was some meaning behind his every word that he wanted her to understand; she could hear it but not interpret it.

"I read about that opera," Lady Odette said. "Eurydice was played by the beautiful Mrs. Westmore, wasn't she?"

Max looked away at last. His gaze landed on his plate. "Yes."

"She is supposed to be a diamond of the first water. No one can stop talking about how beautiful she is. Especially her hair. It is red, isn't it?"

The words slithered through the air even without the help of the exaggerated look Lady Odette gave her.

Almost since the moment he had left Montchampion Manor in August for London, Lady Odette had taunted Ellen that he would set up a mistress. "I am only warning you," she replied when Ellen called her cruel. "A good wife must expect such behavior. I do not want you to be caught unawares."

And everyone knew that Max could not resist a woman with red hair. Had Ellen been blond or brunette or had any other hair color except the intense orange of a flame, he might have written his exposé on Northfield Hall as intended and they would never have married.

An exaggeration. Perhaps even an untruth.

Ellen believed it sometimes, though, especially when she lay awake alone at night, wondering what her husband was doing in London.

"I believe so." Max's tone was suddenly less enthusiastic; his words felt clipped. Almost as if he resented the direction of the conversation.

His mother picked up her glass of wine triumphantly. "She must be very beautiful."

"Well." Max did not look at either of them. He filled his plate with more food than even a man as large as he could possibly eat.

Ellen knew Max loved her. Their marriage was nine years strong, and in that time they had welcomed five children, navigated a life with her family, and become so close that there were days when Ellen could predict Max's words before he even said them.

But things were different at Montchampion Manor. Even before he left for London, Ellen had felt apart from him. Here, he wasn't her husband first and foremost. Here, he was the earl: Lady Odette's son, the household's lord, the man who was supposed to live up to every expectation his father had set out for him.

Neither was Ellen simply his wife anymore. For if Max was the earl, here Ellen was a joke of a countess. She did not command respect; the community did not look to her as a paragon of virtue; nor did she even swan about in fabulous costumes. Instead of being Max's helpmeet, she was an albatross around his neck, earning complaints from his mother and Mr. Nixon and Mrs. Smith that all ended up as Max's problems. And she could not even be a proper wife: ever since Alexander's birth, either her body had been too weak or it had been too dangerous for them to make love. They hadn't touched in four months, but even before that, Max hadn't gotten more than a kiss from Ellen for nearly a year.

Small wonder if the Earl of Meretta kept a mistress in London. Or kissed a ginger-haired singer after drinking too much champagne at the opera.

Ellen would have liked to believe in Max without the shadow of a doubt. But the doubt was there, and while Ellen couldn't pinpoint when it had arrived, she felt it growing larger with every beat of her heart.

"Orpheus does look back at Eurydice," Max said, turning towards her again. "She dies, and he is left with nothing but grief."

"Too bad she must pay the price for his faithlessness." The words came hotly out of her mouth; she could almost feel them burn her lips. Ellen stood. "Excuse me, I don't feel well."

"Ellen!" Max called after her.

She did not look back.

Max pleaded exhaustion to excuse himself from postprandial drinks with Mother. It was not that he wanted to disappoint her, nor that he did not want to spend an hour with her sharing the news from London, nor even that he felt guilty drinking Mother's illicit cordial that she kept in hidden spots throughout the great house.

He needed to speak with Ellen, alone, before the tension between them got any worse.

Though it was true that he really *was* exhausted. As his valet, Downes, helped him change out of his supper jacket and into a night-robe, every muscle in Max's body cried out in protest. Riding by horse was a more comfortable way to travel than within a carriage, but it still left his legs and arse bruised. If he lay down to sleep, he probably wouldn't wake for fifteen hours.

Except he was anxious about Ellen.

He *had* been anxious about Ellen since before he left for London. Definitely since the news reached Northfield Hall that his father had died of a midwinter cold.

If he were to trace it back to its origin, he might have been anxious about Ellen as the Countess of Meretta since the moment he asked her to be his wife. The second time—the first time he hadn't had the presence of mind to think about anything beyond how much he wanted her in his arms forever.

They had always known this phase of their life would come. Yet they had hardly ever talked about it. Max could admit to himself now that he had been afraid to bring it up—afraid, even, to contemplate it in the privacy of his own thoughts. They had been happy at

Northfield Hall. He hadn't wanted to spoil that by worrying about the future.

But now the future was the present. Max was the earl, Ellen was the countess, and somehow, they had to make a life at Montchampion Manor.

Ellen was in her bedchamber when he entered. She hadn't changed out of her evening gown, though she had draped a wool shawl over her shoulders. She knelt by her hearth, her hands tilting to the fire as she whittled a stick into some new shape.

A long time ago, Max had worried he would one day stop finding her beautiful. It had been theoretical, a fear of the unknown beast that was love rather than a fear informed by his own feelings. And in some ways, his attraction to her had changed: he did not feel the urgent need to risk everything in his world in order to claim a kiss, nor did he find every single angle of hers more appealing than that of any other woman in the world.

Yet his heart still yearned for her. He wanted to pluck this moment of her beside the fire, soft light setting her creamy skin aglow and darkening her red hair, from the records of time and preserve it for the next time he had to be apart from her.

His love, it turned out, ran more deeply than he could ever have imagined.

Hearing him, she looked up but didn't say anything.

Max wasn't sure how best to start the conversation. "It is good to be home."

"It is good to have you here." She looked back down at the knife whittling away in her hands.

"How have you been?"

She paused to sweep wood shavings into the hearth with the edge of her hand. Max thought her fingers might end up in the fire; he sucked in a breath as if that would keep her safe.

"There has been some good. The storehouse is open. The beekeeper—Philips, do you remember him?—he was a great help to me in stocking it."

Which meant that for some reason, the footmen who would normally assist had not. Max asked, "And the bad?"

"Mr. Nixon continues to obstruct my every move. He assured me he ordered flax seed for the southern hundred, yet when it came time for planting, he told me the order had failed and so they were 'forced' to plant wheat. And when I told him I was unhappy with his actions, he said, 'We shall wait to see what his lordship thinks,' making it clear as punch what he thinks of *me*." Her knife moved more quickly now. "Mrs. Smith has daily complaints. The new cook is wasting food, the new maids are leaving smudges on the windows, she can't make anyone do their jobs correctly without tea…"

Max knew all of this from her letters. They had already exchanged a half dozen notes about the issue of the crops, and as for the servants, they had known there would be discontent when Ellen announced there would be no tea, coffee, sugar, spices, or other food imported from beyond Britain. "Are you finding time to get to the carpentry workshop?"

She rose to her feet, turning her back to him. Her hands—still holding the stick and the knife—ran across the sides of her head, as if to rake through her hair, except it was tied up in a braid. "When I go, they refuse to tell me what they are working on. They hide the lumber so I cannot even start working on my own project."

When he had left for London, the carpenters had been alarmed by Ellen's interest in helping—and she had given Max a grin, saying, "Let me show them what I can do with a pair of shutters, then ask what they think."

Now, he could hear the tears in her voice, even if she wouldn't show them to him.

"We'll set up your own workshop in the house, then," Max offered. "We have far too many drawing rooms anyhow. Take your pick, and we shall have it converted by the end of the year."

Ellen did not react to this, other than to touch her knife to her stick.

Max tried addressing one of her other concerns: "I am reviewing the property with Nixon tomorrow. I'll sort him out."

Finally putting down her knife and figurine, Ellen found a handkerchief and blew her nose. "You would do better to turn him out."

"His family has been stewards to our land for over a hundred years." More to the point, Max needed Nixon if he had any hope of running Montchampion Manor successfully. Still, if the man continued to be so impolitic as to ignore Ellen's instructions, he could not remain for long.

Ellen turned back in his direction, her arms crossing her stomach as if to hug herself. "Well, and how have you been?"

A hundred answers rushed to his tongue. He had saved up so many anecdotes from London: the insanity of Queen Caroline's trial, gossip from the parties and salons, how bewildering it was to be in the House of Lords compared to the House of Commons, anecdotes from his breakfasts with her father.

He wanted to share them all with Ellen. At the moment, however, he couldn't stand to spend a single moment more without touching her.

"I have missed you." Max held out a hand, palm open, inviting her to join him.

Ellen smiled. But it was sad, and instead of coming to him, she turned away again. "I am fatigued."

Too fatigued to hold his hand? He let it fall back to his side.

They were no strangers to interrupting their bodies' intimacy. Ever since Alexander's birth a year ago, which had nearly killed Ellen, Max had been avoiding kisses too deep.

Still, they had been apart for months. All he wanted to do was touch her.

He said, "You should rest, then."

"You too. You have been traveling all day."

They stood in silence together for a moment longer. At Northfield Hall, they had only had the one bed. Here, they each had their own bedroom suite. They hadn't yet set a pattern for whose bed they slept in.

It didn't occur to Max that he wouldn't sleep in the same room as Ellen that night until she walked away from him, towards her own bed, and said, "Goodnight, then. I'll see you in the morning."

He was too shocked to do anything but agree. "Yes. Sleep well. The morning will be better."

For a moment, he believed himself: they were both tired and overwhelmed. In the morning, they would kiss and eat breakfast with the children and feel like normal again.

Then the door shut behind him, and he was alone in his bedroom. Back after four months away, and she hadn't so much as touched him.

That wasn't something a simple night's sleep could fix. But for the time being, a night's sleep was all Max could conjure.

The Tour

Ellen debated how best to ask to join Max on his tour of the estate with Mr. Nixon. After last night, she didn't dare creep into his room for breakfast without permission. She should have put all her doubts aside and kissed him like she had been longing to do for months, but somehow, she couldn't quiet the fear in her heart. For their whole conversation, all she could hear was the sound of his voice seducing another woman. And when she opened her mouth, she couldn't seem to say anything she meant. All she could manage to do was complain.

Things were not right at Montchampion Manor, and it turned out that Max's return did not solve the ache in her heart.

She hoped his presence would do more to solve the rest of the problems at the estate. Which was why, after waking far too early and worrying far too much about how to ask his permission, she decided to simply dress for riding and show up at the stables to join Max on his tour.

Mr. Nixon was already there, holding too tightly to his mare's reins as he expounded upon drainage. When Ellen appeared, he silenced himself, as if the explanation of a ditch might offend her ears.

"I thought I would come along," Ellen said to Max.

He ran his eyes across her without expression. Ellen was struck by the exhaustion written on his face: dark circles under his eyes, deeper lines around his mouth, and a certain hang of his head that told her he needed sleep.

It used to be he could go days without a proper night's rest and still look like an Adonis. His age, she supposed, was catching up with him.

"If I may, my lady, it will be a strenuous ride," said Mr. Nixon. Whenever he spoke to her in front of Max—or Lady Odette, for that matter—he put on a sickly sweet manner, as if she were no older than Rosalind and in need of firm guidance. "Perhaps you would prefer to ride with one of the groomsmen to the castle."

The castle being one of several inane follies "decorating" the thousand acres of Montchampion Manor. It was at the estate's highest elevation, and when one climbed to the top of its three-story tower, one had a view of the sea to the east.

When Ellen had first arrived as countess, she would have replied to Mr. Nixon with as much kindness as she could muster. Now, she didn't waste her breath.

She looked to Max instead. The only person in the whole county whom Mr. Nixon might actually listen to.

He lowered his chin. "If you feel up to it, my lady, I welcome your company."

They had to wait for a groom to saddle her horse, which meant standing around awkwardly in the stable yard. Ellen pressed her lips together to keep from saying much as Mr. Nixon invented more ways to discourage her from joining. "We shall be gone much of the day. Does Mrs. Smith know you will not be present to answer any household questions?" and "The men in the fields do not always watch their language, my lord. Perhaps it would be better if Lady Meretta only joins us as we review the ornamental garden?"

The fact that Max hadn't yet summarily dismissed the man—had even defended him, merely on the basis of *tradition*—helped fortify Ellen against the assault. The man had been treating her to such displays of belittlement for four months without Max's presence to leash him in. In a way, Ellen was glad to let him go on, if only to prove to Max what she had dealt with.

At last, Max said, "You are overly concerned with Lady Meretta, Mr. Nixon. Pray do not let it distract you from our duties today."

His icy cold tone made him sound like his father, who had protected conservative order above all else. That part, Ellen didn't enjoy.

The way it silenced Mr. Nixon and made his eyes turn into narrow little beads gave her immense satisfaction.

When at last her horse was ready, Max waved away the groom and helped her into the saddle himself. His hands on her waist sent a jolt of warmth through her body. She had forgotten how steady his fingers felt even when they did nothing except guide her in place.

Every ounce of her soul begged for him to not let go, to in fact pull her down from the mare and hold her against his chest.

She settled into her sidesaddle position as if she didn't feel a thing. But his hands trailed down the sides of her legs, and when she glanced down, he was waiting solemnly for her look. His lips twitched into something of a smile. "It was a good idea for you to join us."

It was sad that in this new life of hers, she had so needed to hear her husband affirm that.

Montchampion Manor was too large to review in a single day, so they spent the morning focused on the most critical area: the fields where Nixon had planted wheat despite Ellen's instructions to replace it with flax.

"The seeds would have gone to waste," Nixon said, after spending a quarter hour needlessly explaining the planting process. "We have spent generations developing the perfect wheat strain, and if we had not sown them this season, we would have lost the strain forever. The flax will keep for next year."

The day was chill and gray, even for November, with a wind whipping in from the coast that cut through Max's woolen layers.

At the moment, one couldn't tell there was *anything* planted in the fields spreading beyond them, much less differentiate between wheat and flax.

Max looked over to Ellen to see her reaction to Nixon's defense. Her cheeks and nose were red from the cold. Her mare kept drifting a few steps away from them, and Ellen—who had never had a horse of her own before and was only a passable rider—couldn't seem to bring her back to the pack.

She still managed to fix an austere—almost countess-like—glare upon Nixon. "What will change between this year and next to prevent you from making the same argument?"

Nixon ducked his chin obsequiously. "We shall have more than a few months to plan, my lady."

Shortcake shifted beneath Max; even the horse could pick up on the tension simmering between Ellen and Nixon.

Max tried to observe the conflict as an objective outside party might. On the one hand, Nixon was charged with caring for Montchampion Manor and had, for the last few decades, been accustomed to making decisions about its profitability with very little guidance from Max's father. The manor harvested and sold a staggering amount of wheat each year, which supplied the family coffers with plenty of money and earned Nixon a generous annual salary. A rational man *would* resist switching from a crop as valuable as gold.

On the other hand, Ellen was determined to turn Montchampion Manor into a community like Northfield Hall. She needed fields of flax so they could begin producing linen, which would replace the cotton and silks the estate currently imported for textiles. Moreover, she needed a steward she could count on.

And where did he, the new Earl of Meretta, stand in this conflict? He looked at the fields again. He had spent his boyhood on rides like this with his father and Nixon—and how he had hated when they inserted adult questions into his daydreams about the clouds and fairy maidens running across the fields to greet him!

When they had married, Max had promised Ellen that once he inherited, they would make over Montchampion Manor in the style of Northfield Hall. He had meant it; he still meant it.

He just didn't expect it to happen in the first six months, or even the first year. In a decade, perhaps, they would be able to survey the land and see every corner of it put to use for the common good.

The problem was that Ellen expected change to happen overnight.

The other problem was that Nixon kept ignoring her.

Max didn't blame the steward if he didn't like the changes Ellen proposed. But he would not stand for a man who disrespected his wife. "Next year, we shall make sure we have a plan several months in advance so all necessary preparations will be made. We shall also be clear that Lady Meretta's instructions are to be heeded as if they came from my own mouth."

Nixon looked away with a quiet, barely audible "Yes, sir."

Ellen didn't meet his eyes either. Her lips closed in a flat, disappointed line, and he knew that in her view, he wasn't doing enough.

She wanted him to dismiss Nixon without a moment's delay. Anything else allied him more with the status quo than with her.

She didn't understand they were playing a game of politics, and that it was more delicate than any patchy compromise he had ever built in Parliament. Montchampion Manor was a larger institution than Northfield Hall; over a thousand people relied on it for some kind of income, from the household servants to the groundsworkers to the tenant farmers and village tradespeople.

When Lord Preston had transformed Northfield Hall, his household already trusted him and the larger community didn't have any opinion one way or another how he ran his business.

Max had just arrived as the earl after years of estrangement from his family. No one at the manor house trusted him, not even his mother. They all thought he had been living a strange, dangerous life at Northfield Hall, where none of the proper order of the world was observed. Max knew exactly what they imagined about Northfield Hall because he once had, too: that it was a haven for criminals, that it was as dangerous as the Seven Dials in London, that it was as full of hedonists as of do-gooders.

Already, the bulk of the household had quit when Ellen forbade further imports of tea and coffee. A steady stream of laborers, too, kept giving notice that instead of working the next harvest, they were headed to London to try their luck at some other employment.

Max needed time to prove to Montchampion Manor that he was not there to sell their souls to the devil. He was their leader by birthright, but he needed to earn their trust so he could do more than order them about.

If they didn't win over the people who relied upon Montchampion Manor already, then what was the point in trying to share their wealth with them?

"Excellent," Max said to his dissatisfied audience. "Let's move on before the rain arrives."

The Luncheon

By the time they returned at half past two, Ellen's bones ached. She wasn't made for horse riding. Nor had her flannel petticoats managed to protect her skin from taking on the November chill. She couldn't keep from shivering as she and Max walked together back into the manor house.

To call it a manor house was something like calling champagne a simple grape juice. Yes, the "manor house" was a home to the earl's family, but it was far more a palace than a house ever could be. Its exterior façade resembled a Roman temple; its entryway spanned a hundred square feet and was made entirely of marble; its forty rooms stretched across three wings and were lit by two hundred pristine glass windows. Several of its ceilings boasted gilded paintings, and one sitting room's walls were entirely covered in red velvet.

If they opened its doors to common folk, it could house all of the local village and then some.

Max led her inside through a side entrance into a portrait gallery. At the far end—far enough away that they were dark smudges to

Ellen's eyes—two maids scurried from the windows they had been washing and into some other room, to give Max and Ellen privacy.

Mrs. Smith was very strict about that rule, even though Ellen had said several times she did not want the servants to feel as if they were invisible. Without them, her life would not function as it needed to; she wanted to acknowledge them, know their names, ask after their families.

A hard thing to do when they were constantly disappearing.

"Are you hungry?" The click of Max's boots echoed through the long room.

"Yes." Her stomach had been growling for the better part of an hour, but she hadn't wanted to say anything that might give Mr. Nixon a reason to send her back on her own.

"Shall we have a meal sent up to our rooms?"

Once upon a time, that invitation would have been suggestive, and they would have snuck off for an hour or two in bed with each other.

Now, she couldn't imagine he thought there was any hope of that kind of bliss. She was exhausted, she was grumpy, and they hadn't touched except for that moment when he had helped her onto her horse.

He was inviting her to privacy, perhaps conversation, nothing more.

"I'd like to check on the children first."

"I'll come with you. By the time we are finished, our trays should be waiting for us."

He found one of the disappearing maids as they exited the gallery and gave the necessary instructions. Together, they climbed the three stories of silk-carpeted stairs to the nursery. It stretched through a suite of five rooms, including a schoolroom, a playroom, and three bedrooms. Ellen had spent most of her first few months at Montchampion Manor hiding up here, under the excuse that the children needed her presence as they adjusted to their new home.

The truth had been the reverse. In a home where the housekeeper still obeyed her mother-in-law, the servants walked away rather than trust her, and the neighbors dispensed polite sneers when they made their calls, Ellen had only felt safe when upstairs with her children or locked away in her bedroom with Max.

It was a little better now. If Montchampion Manor had to be her home, Ellen was determined not to allow herself to be alienated in it. Still, she breathed a sigh of relief each time she crossed into the nursery.

The three girls, delighted at having their father home, flocked to Max first. Ellen crossed to where Nurse Kathleen sat in a rocker with the littlest ones, Robert and Alexander. Ellen took one-year-old Alex into her arms and sank to the floor so Robert could tell her all about the wood blocks in front of him.

Their visit with the children was brief. Little Odette and the boys were about to lie down for their naps, and Rosalind and Amelia were expected to practice their reading. Quick as it was, it breathed some life into Ellen. By the time she and Max arrived to the luncheon on the little table in his private sitting room, she almost felt ready to have an honest conversation with her husband.

"Tell me the truth," she said as she served a slice of roast pig onto each of their plates. "What would Mr. Nixon need to do for you to dismiss him?"

Max poured himself a glass of elderberry wine. "Ellen, it isn't as simple as you see it."

"I have tried to see it from your view. His family has been stewards of this land for generations. Keeping him here is keeping the order necessary to the proper functioning of Montchampion Manor. Yet isn't part of that order obedience to the rule of those superior to you? I must answer to you, but surely Mr. Nixon must answer to me." She was careful not to sound hard-done-by or mocking. She really was trying to understand why everyone was so threatened by her suggestions for change. She didn't want to be as blind to their sensibilities as they were to hers. "Why, then, is he not dismissed?"

"We must go softly." Max cut longer and harder into his meat than necessary. It splintered under his force, tough little pieces of ham falling about his plate. "We must not make too many changes too fast. Mr. Nixon knows this land better than I do. I need him here, at least for a full year, or else I won't know enough about the estate to make wise decisions. Which of the fields always floods in the spring? Where is the ground too sandy to grow anything, and is that why we built a folly there? Who of our tradespeople can be trusted, and who will cut too many corners? These are all things you and I must learn before we can upend everything."

"Mr. Nixon cannot be the only person who knows such things."

Max sighed. "I don't like the way he speaks to you, either."

There was that, at least. Ellen focused on her own food; the meat was tough. "You seem to be the only one with any power to do something about it. And yet you don't do enough."

"I will be firmer with him. It is only my first morning home." His face was so lined with exhaustion that he almost looked like an old man. His eyes closed, then opened again. "I know it has been hard to be here alone. I'm sorry I had to be gone for so long."

It had been harder than hard. It had been lonely and infuriating.

Before, when Ellen would send Max off to London, she had always known he would hurry home as soon as he finished his parliamentary agenda.

This time, it had felt more like they had said goodbye sometime before he actually left. She had lost her husband when he became the earl, and he had yet to return.

She wondered again, as she had a dozen times these past few months, ever since Lady Odette had thrown it in her face, whether Max had set himself up with a companion in London.

Better not to think about it. "Did you finish the business at the bank? Have you divested from the usual investments?"

Most of the earl's funds had been invested in bank stocks or shipping shares. Except those stocks and shares grew by capitalizing on trade between Britain, its colonies, and slave territories.

Max had promised one of his first priorities was to change the way their money was invested. Otherwise every single thing Ellen purchased made her feel dirty. "I did, much to my agent's dismay."

"Thank you."

Her focus returned to her plate. Max, however, reached out and placed his hand over hers.

Their fingers were bare, and his palm was as cold as hers. "You don't need to thank me. I did not do it as a favor to you. I believe in this too, Ellen. You do know that, don't you?"

Before he had inherited, back when they had spent their nights nuzzling each other at Northfield Hall, Ellen would have said she had known it as well as she knew her own beating heart.

She wished she still had that certainty. But in the six months since they had moved here, it felt like he had more often sided with his mother or Mrs. Smith or Mr. Nixon than he had affirmed her decisions. When Lady Odette complained that Ellen forbade sugar, he asked if they could make an exception for his mother. When the head butler quit on account of the lack of tea, Max had tried to negotiate with her about allowing the household to use up its existing stores. When the carpenters told Mr. Nixon they were uncomfortable with her in their workshop, Max had asked if she wouldn't be more comfortable doing woodwork on her own somewhere inside the great house.

Ellen didn't know if she could actually believe Max now. She wanted to, though, so she squeezed his fingers and replied, "I know."

Max clung to Ellen's fingers even after she relaxed her hold on him.

This reunion of theirs was too hard. They were spending too much time *discussing* things and too little time *reuniting*. This act of intertwining his fingers with hers was the most intimate act they had shared since he had left in August.

It would not do.

"The opera I mentioned last night has stayed with me. I keep thinking about why Orpheus could not trust that Eurydice was following him." In truth, it made Max think of when he and Ellen had first met. She discovered he was lying to her, and instead of threatening to blackmail him or turn him into the authorities, she made him promise to do better or else she would *never forgive him*.

He had never known faith like that before. She was Orpheus, only she never looked back. She trusted, blindly, that Max would prove he was worth her trust.

From the first moment she bestowed him with her faith, Max had clung to it like a drowning man to a raft.

"Perhaps because he knew that if he were in her position, he would have run off with Aristaeus, rather than flee at his own peril."

Ellen withdrew her fingers. She put them to use immediately, holding fork in one hand and knife in the other to slice a potato in two.

Max wished she had kept holding onto him. "Looking back will never reassure him. No matter whether she has stopped following or not; if he looks back, he will kill her. So why does he do it? What human instinct forces him to literally turn on her?"

Ellen, who had been chewing throughout his musings, suddenly looked pale. She grew still, like a frozen tableau of a woman eating. "Are you trying to confess to something?"

"Confess?" Max almost stuttered. The question was so surprising. Did Ellen object to the opera, and had Max completely forgotten? Had there been some incident at the opera she thought he had been a part of?

What in good logic could the opera have to do with a confession?

Ellen held up a hand to freeze whatever he might say next. "I don't think I want to know. Your mother says I should, that if I were a good wife I would be aware and make sure not to host awkward supper parties. But I don't think I can stand it. Oh, please, don't tell me."

Max had no idea what she was saying, but he could tell she was fighting to keep from crying. Her eyes were bright red.

And what did his mother have to do with anything?

"Ellen." Max reached for her, intending to fold her into his arms, but she flinched away.

Whatever this was, she clearly held him at fault.

"My love, I haven't any idea what you are talking about." He thought about going through his list of guesses. But they were both tired, and they were not newlyweds. He had learned better than to spend hours trying to imagine what was going on in Ellen's head. "Won't you speak plainly?"

She angled her whole body away from him. "The opera singer. Mrs. Westmore. Or whomever it is you've been keeping. I don't want to know about it."

At last—with great horror—Max understood.

Had his own mother put this idea in Ellen's head?

How was he to get it out?

"Ellen, I'm not keeping anyone." He reached for her again, and this time, she didn't shy away. Still, Max limited himself to curling a palm around her forearm. "I never have, and I never will. You are my wife. I need no one else."

Her whole body was shaking. "I know it is done. It is expected of you, even. And she has red hair..." The words disappeared into a wail. Ellen lifted her free hand to catch the tears escaping her eyes.

Max pulled his chair beside hers. "You are all I want. I saw Mrs. Westmore on stage and once at a party. I didn't even speak to her. That is the sum of it."

"Someone else then. I don't want to know who." She groped blindly for a napkin, but hers was in her lap already soiled. Max pulled the handkerchief from his pocket and placed it in her fingers.

"No one. There is no one."

"But..." At last she turned back to him, even if her eyes only landed on his shoulder instead of meeting his. "What with the doctor's prohibition...it would be understandable. I can't, after all."

Alexander's birth had been difficult. One might even describe it as dangerous: it lasted almost three days, and the accoucheur had begun warning Max that Ellen might die with the baby. Somehow, both she and Alexander had survived, but the physician—and a midwife Ellen consulted, and their brother-in-law John Anderson—all warned that Ellen might not survive another birth.

The most obvious way to avoid that was to avoid impregnating her.

"We have not properly discussed it." They had, in fact, avoided the topic altogether. At first, it had been because Ellen had needed so much time to recover from the pregnancy—and there had been a new baby to adore. Then Max's father had died. They had moved to Montchampion Manor. There had always been so many things to do and decisions to make that when they did kiss, Max drew away before he could get too excited, and aside from apologetic smiles to each other, they never talked about what was happening.

Max hadn't supposed there would be any consequences to that.

"Nor have we properly explored it." Max dared wrap his other arm across Ellen now so that she nestled against his chest and he could rest his cheek upon her hair. "I *have* been thinking about what we can do about it. But I swear to you, Ellen, I have been faithful to you."

She trembled.

Max asked, even though there was only one answer he could bear to hear, "Do you believe me?"

For a long time, she didn't answer. Max shut his eyes and ignored every instinct to badger her for an answer—or change the subject. He waited.

"I'm all mixed up," Ellen said at last. She turned in his arms and looped her elbows around his neck. Her cheek pressed against his. "I want to believe you. Give me some time, and I am sure I will."

Eyes still closed, Max nuzzled against her. He wished that didn't sound so bleak. He had never broken his marriage vows—had never even been tempted to—and so at least in this, he knew he deserved Ellen's ferocious faith.

He didn't know if he could survive losing it after all this time.

Ellen was hardly aware of the physical world. Her cheeks were wet, her nose running, her limbs trembling. Max's jaw was prickly against her face. These things she *knew*, yet she barely registered them.

She was too caught up in trying to sort out how she felt. These last four months, she had been so busy forcing herself to trust Max that she hadn't realized that she actually believed what Lady Odette suggested. When he started going on again about the opera, Ellen had known with a certainty deep in her bones what he wanted to tell her—that he related to Orpheus, who had killed his own wife by listening to some terrible instinct, because he, too, had given in to his baser urges.

Did she believe him? Ellen didn't know how to get back to that kind of confidence. She believed that he didn't want her to be upset; she believed that he would pivot from confession to denial; she even believed that he loved her as much as always, despite anything that he may have done with some other woman.

She had spent too much time picturing exactly how he would arrange an affair in London. This was a man who, before they married, carried on with paramours all the time. He had even been in the gossip columns for stealing away the prime minister's mistress!

It would be so easy for him to find a woman to keep him company in London. Even if it wasn't a protracted relationship. It might have been just one night, when he was feeling particularly desolate and when Ellen seemed particularly far away.

Once she had started imagining it, Ellen had realized how easy it would be for Max. How obvious that he would do it!

How could she now believe that, given the opportunity to dally with any number of women without needing to see Ellen the next morning, Max had *not* had an affair?

She pulled away to clean up her nose with the handkerchief. Max's hands drifted down to her hips, but he didn't let go of her. He touched his forehead to hers. "Will you let me know when I am allowed to kiss you again?"

Fool that she was, in spite of everything, all Ellen wanted was for Max to kiss her. She needed it as much as she needed him to swear he had never so much as looked at another woman.

And she needed it to come from him.

"You're allowed." She wiped her nose one more time to make sure it was not dripping.

Then Max's lips were upon hers. He started gently, a few soft kisses against her mouth. Ellen raised a hand to his jaw, a signal they had used for years now to make everything more intense. Max leaned forward. Mouth still on hers—a little more roughly now, with a little less care—he gripped her hips and lifted her onto his lap.

He was already as hard as steel.

He opened his mouth, his teeth nipping her lips. His chin scraped against her skin. Ellen plunged her fingers under his coat and shirt, down across the rippled muscles of his back, towards his buttocks.

They had treated each other with too much care for far too long. Ellen wanted to be fucked as if she were nothing but the object of his desire.

She wanted so badly to *be* the object of his desire.

Max's hands found her arse now and squeezed. Ellen whimpered, which she turned into a hiss. "What are you going to do with me, now that you have me?"

His reply was to stand up. Suddenly Ellen was in the air, supported by nothing except Max's strength. She wrapped her legs around his waist, her breasts and stomach pressed tight against his chest. Max kissed her again with mouth and tongue and teeth.

The way he had once in the middle of a rainstorm, when they were determined to have nothing to do with each other.

Then he walked with her across the room. He slammed her against the wall—with just enough care that the impact titillated her every nerve and didn't hurt her at all. He lifted one hand from her arse to her hair; still kissing her, he shook out her braid. When he had a palmful of hair spread across his fingers, he pressed his nose into it. "This is the only red hair that makes me wild."

She didn't believe him. For the moment, she didn't care. "What are you going to do about it?"

"What do you want me to do about it?" he growled into her neck.

"I want you to fuck me." But he couldn't. "I want you to fuck me like you always have."

"As you wish." Max claimed her mouth once more. Ellen wondered if he really meant it; would he lift her skirts next and throw himself inside her, consequences be damned?

If he didn't spend inside her, perhaps it would work.

"I shall fuck you," Max promised. His lips had moved to her ear now, his voice once again low and gravelly. "But not exactly like I always have."

And then he stepped away from her. Ellen was fully dressed, not even a button of her gown undone, yet the air rushing between them pricked her skin with goose pimples.

Max's fingers drifted down from her hair to catch her hand in his. Grinning at her, he tugged her away from the wall. "I did some shopping in London. Come see what I got for you."

Ellen followed him through the door that led from his sitting room into his dressing room. A trunk sat near the narrow window, lid lifted. Max let go of her hand to bend over it, remove a false bottom, and withdraw a velvet box.

"What is that?" For a terrible moment, Ellen feared he had bought her pearls from China. But when Max lifted the lid, there were no jewels inside.

Only a slim wooden phallus.

It was made from cherry and had been sanded down and polished to a perfect, satiny finish. As a carved object, it was beautiful.

As a present from her husband, it was puzzling.

She changed her question: "Where did you get that?"

"From a special seller in London. It is so I can still fuck you without any fear of risking a child."

The excitement that had propelled her through the room with him cooled. "What gave you the idea for such a thing?" This was, after all, no drawing room topic. Had he spilled out his troubles to the lovely courtesan who provided distraction while advising him on how to save his marital bed?

Max's smile dimmed. "I consulted with a friend."

"A friend?" Ellen was glad she hadn't taken off any clothes. It would make it easier to storm out of the room. "A female friend, perhaps? One who knows all sorts of ways to please a man and not get with child in the meantime?"

"No!" Max squeezed shut his eyes and heaved a sigh. "No, it was a gentleman friend. Ellen, I was trying to do something good for you."

She didn't believe him. Yet she had promised she would try, so Ellen considered that he might be telling the truth.

Unfortunately, it didn't make the story much better. "And to which gentleman did you decide to disclose our troubles?"

"I didn't disclose much. It was a general topic of conversation."

He still didn't look her in the eye. "It matters to me what was said to whom, when, and in what context. Most importantly, I should like to know *why*."

Max set the phallus, still in its box, on a shelf. He paced in a tiny circle. Anger curled through every muscle of his body, and Ellen braced herself for a misdirection or a lie or a vicious argument.

Especially when he smacked his palm against the wall.

Yet when he turned back to her, he confessed: "I went to White's Club after sessions ended."

In her darkest moments, Ellen had pictured him at all sorts of brothels or disreputable salons.

Going to White's was a betrayal that stood on its own. He might as well have taken an advertisement in the newspaper to announce that he preferred the company of reprobates to that of the Preston family.

Ellen steeled herself for what might come next in his confession.

"I did this on a few evenings, even though I know you don't approve of the gentlemen who keep membership there. It is a decent supper, and more importantly, it is where unofficial decisions are made about committees and chairs and all that. I don't wager on ladies' reputations, nor do I join in any investments of an unsavory nature."

That, at least, Ellen could believe.

"In any case, one evening, after a few bottles of scotch had been consumed by us all, the conversation turned to wives and bedsport and whatnot. It turns out that I am not the only gentleman who has been warned to leave his lady alone. We…commiserated. I do not like to tell you who exactly brought up the idea of the phallus, for it would betray his wife's identity. He is one of the fellows who decided to take up a mistress as his solution, so he only knows about the phallus because he walked in on his wife with *her* lover and saw they were using it.

"That gave me the idea, and I started asking around the way one does when looking for something illicit, and I found this phallus.

"As to *why*—" Max suddenly propelled himself from the window. In an instant, he loomed over her, and his demeanor was much angrier than it had been before. "You are my wife, Ellen. I intend to fuck you by every method available to me for as long as I live."

Her whole body quivered. All thoughts of White's and women disappeared.

She didn't care about believing him or berating him.

She only wanted him to follow through on that promise.

Max ran a lone, rough finger down the side of her cheek. It landed between her lips. "Would you like to try it out, or not?"

"I would."

Max ignored his instinct to kiss her and fetched the phallus instead. Excitement began to take over his body again, which was good, because he didn't know how to handle the fear that had begun to swirl in his stomach. If Ellen didn't believe him...or if Ellen thought him perverted for buying the phallus in the first place!

He didn't need to pursue those thoughts. She wanted to try it. She stood still, cheeks in high color, basically panting for him to show her what to do next.

Max was excited, and he need not admit any other emotions.

He led her by the hand into his bedroom. Against the post of the bed, he kissed her—not for long, just enough to return the taste of her to his lips. His cock pulsed against the stricture of his trousers, but he let it go ignored for now.

Instead, he undressed Ellen. Her gowns were never complicated: just a few buttons here, some drawstrings there, and pull everything over her head to make her naked. He took his time with it anyhow. He particularly liked to watch her breasts move—almost transform—as he loosened the corset and untied the strings keeping everything in place.

They were much larger than they had been when he married her. Droopier, too, which meant there was even more of a show to watch when he undressed her. When Max finally threw off the last of her clothes, he indulged himself in scooping the breasts up in his hands and kissing her mouth.

He had missed that.

But this was not about following the script they both knew so well. That was too easy—and too dangerous.

Max did not allow himself to do what usually came next, which was strip himself, climb onto the bed, and see who would mount whom first.

Instead, he stepped far enough back to break the kiss. He lifted Ellen at the waist—she let out a delicious gasp—and set her on the mattress. Then he placed the phallus in her hand.

"Feel it. Touch it. Think about what you want to do with it."

She began by stroking it with her fingers. She rubbed her thumb along its grain in that old, familiar way she had of touching wood. Still sitting up, she brought it to her chest and ran its tip across the peaks of her nipples.

Max had to take a ragged breath.

Ellen lifted her gaze, locking eyes with him. She didn't break off even as she scooted backward on the bed and lowered onto her back. She brought the phallus to her face now, holding it at its base and stroking its hooded tip along her cheek.

Max could hardly take it. "Put it in your mouth."

She smiled at him, as if to tease, then obeyed. Her lips opened in a circle, and her tongue darted out to guide the phallus inside. Max didn't have thoughts anymore, only need, and what he needed was to touch her, to take her, to fuck her.

He joined her on the bed. He had to shrug off his coat for movement, but other than that, he didn't allow himself to remove any clothes. When he lay on his belly, his cock pressed strongly—and a little painfully—against his body. He ignored it and nestled between Ellen's knees. "Keep playing with it," he told her, and then, anchoring himself with hands on her hips, he plunged his mouth into her quim.

This, too, was a little different in shape and size than when Max had first met her, but it tasted the same. He tilted his head so he could watch her suck the phallus—for she still did, her eyes stubbornly on him—while he toyed with her valleys. He knew he had found the right pattern when the phallus fell with her hand to her side and her head tipped back, her eyes screwing shut.

Max focused on doing more of the same, for as long as it took. He imagined the look on her face when the orgasm broke; he predicted the victory that would flood his body; he reveled in the feel of his cock throbbing as he licked and kissed his wife and wondered if maybe, just maybe, the experience alone would make him come in his trousers at the very same moment that she came on his tongue.

She didn't quite orgasm. He recognized the breaths, the anticipation, and then the frustration as each coursed through her body. It had happened before, even when every moment of the night had lined up to bring her perfect pleasure. Max paused. "Bad luck?"

Ellen nodded. "It felt good anyhow." She looked down at him, a little smirk on her lips. "I wish you were inside me."

"Then it is time to put this to its original purpose." Max took the phallus from her hand. Rolling off the bed, he crossed to his armoire, where he had tucked away a vial of oil for this purpose. He returned to Ellen and knelt beside her as he slowly rubbed the oil onto the phallus.

"May I do that to you at the same time?" Her hand landed on his trousers even as she asked. Max didn't have breath for a moment; he nodded so that she would reach beneath the clothes and free his poor cock at last.

"But I am not going inside you," he reminded her. Reminded himself. In his hands, the phallus was growing warm and slick.

In Ellen's hands, his cock was as hard and hot as could be.

"Not inside my quim, anyway," Ellen said, but Max didn't understand her because he was fast dissolving into nothing but sexual pleasure.

He forced himself to focus on the phallus—the wooden one—and her legs, which still lay apart, her quim pink and quivering in need. "Are you ready?" he asked.

"Are you?" she replied, and then she tilted back her head, pausing her hand on his cock for a moment as he slid the phallus inside her body.

He had bought a slim version because he wasn't sure what it would feel like for Ellen and didn't want to hurt her. Now, he wished he had gotten one at least as thick as his own cock. She moaned at its first touch, and he could see her quim tightening around it, as if to pull and keep it inside of her.

He knew what that felt like on his own skin. He was amazed it could feel just as scintillating to watch it on this object.

He had positioned it so its wooden balls hung below her opening, same as if he had been fucking her with his body, but after a few strokes, Ellen reached down and rotated the phallus. Now the balls teased against the rest of her quim as he teased her with thrusts. Pink pleasure ran across her skin, and again, she leaned back her head, her eyes screwed tightly shut.

"It is almost perfect," she whispered.

"Faster? Deeper? Harder?" Max couldn't have formed a full sentence if he tried; his trousers had fallen down to his knees and his cock hung in the air at a severe angle, almost purple with anger at being ignored.

"More you." Eyes flying open, Ellen looked at him fiercely for one moment, as if daring him to contradict her. Then, rising onto her elbows, she leaned over and took his cock inside her mouth.

Max almost forgot to operate the phallus. Ellen's tongue and cheeks were so soft, so wet, so warm. Everything a cock could want. She tightened the seal of her lips and sucked, massaging him with strokes that matched the pace of the wooden toy inside her. Max couldn't keep track of what was happening or who was doing what or how the pleasure ended up exploding through him.

He only knew it did. It coursed through him like liquid gold. It released a tension he had been holding for months. It lasted forever. It couldn't last long enough.

When Max opened his eyes, he discovered that Ellen, too, was coming, her hips bucking wildly against the phallus even though he had let go of it. His seed had spilled across her, splattering her cheek and hair and chest. When she saw him watching her, she grinned.

"That was the best we've done in years."

He flopped onto the mattress beside her and pulled her into the profile of his body. "Do you forgive me?"

"For what?"

"For going to White's."

"Oh." She rolled onto her side, allowing his knees to tuck behind hers. "Yes. I understand."

It wasn't exactly the absolution he craved. "Do you believe me?"

This time, she didn't ask for further explanation. She pulled his palms so they rested on each one of her breasts, and she burrowed her head against the mattress. After that—after a long moment—she said, "I am trying to."

He hated that he couldn't ask for more. Max held her close and, eventually, fell asleep.

The Tea

His mother sent word via her maid Petit, who communicated with Max's man Downes, that she would like to take tea with Max. Downes had the decency to redden at the phrasing, knowing as he did that Max abided by Ellen's abolition of tea when at home. "I shall join her," Max instructed the man to reply, "but I shall expect peppermint tea."

Nevertheless, his mother had all the accoutrements for tea assembled when he reported to her private sitting room. The porcelain had been purchased personally for her by a friend who visited China, the glassware had been imported from Venice, and the ivory bowl enshrining the mound of sugar was directly from the coast of Africa.

This was not the scene of a woman trying to adapt to a new, export-less lifestyle.

Max allowed her polite chitchat for the first quarter hour. Even though he had spent the last decade all but estranged from her, Max still knew his mother well, and he knew this was as much a display of loneliness as it was of rebellion. He would give her the company she craved.

But when she brought up the theater—when she actually said "I am envious that you got to see the great Mrs. Westmore. Mrs. Spurrier wrote me that her husband has been to see the opera three times because he is so captivated by her singing"—Max could not indulge his mother any longer.

"Tell me why, Mother, you would plant in Ellen's mind the idea that I was carrying on with Mrs. Westmore when you have no evidence to suggest such a thing."

She hid her shock well. She poured herself another tea and shaved sugar into it as if she would never have the chance to eat sugar again. "I do not need to have *evidence* to know that my son is intrigued by a talented singer with fire-colored hair. Neither should your wife; she should know you well enough to understand you without you needing to say a word."

"It is dangerous to cast aspersions on a man's character based on nothing but your..." For lack of a better word, Max finished, "intuition."

Mother pursed her lips over her cup but did not drink. "What is this, 'aspersions'?"

There were times, like now, when she thickened her French accent and pretended not to know a definition, all to help her win an argument. Max considered calling her bluff, but instead played along. "Sullying my character. Blackening my reputation. Besmirching my honor."

"But how is it to besmirch your honor to understand your nature? You are apart from your wife for months at a time. Of course you will find someone beautiful to keep you company. This is not a black mark upon a man's honor." Then, placing her undrunk tea back on the table, she raised a single eyebrow at him. "Unless you plan to separate from Lady Meretta for this singer."

Perhaps it was true that no one thought twice about a gentleman setting up a lover in addition to his wife. Max certainly didn't consider his friends villains, and half of them had dalliances outside their marriages.

But he didn't live by society's code. He lived by Ellen's. "I have no relationship with this singer, nor with any woman except my wife. By suggesting otherwise, you have made her doubt me. I should like to know why you think that is a kind thing to do to your own son."

"Do not speak to me in such tones." She fixed him with a glare until Max bowed his head in silent apology. Then, spreading her hands across her silk skirt, she explained: "I feel for poor Ellen, if you must know. She is so ill prepared to be Lady Meretta. When I married your father, I did not understand English manners, but at least I knew what it was to be a countess. Your wife...she does not seem to understand. She thinks being lady of the house means doing whatever she wants. Spending her days in the carpentry workshop! I am trying to help her, Max. She cannot change the world to suit her desires. She must learn her place in the world. And she must not make unnatural demands of you. You are not a mere *husband*. You are an *earl*. Your duty is to the king and to the realm. Her duty is to support you. Which includes not making a fuss when you take up with a pretty companion."

The most dangerous part of his mother's speech was how its familiarity tugged at him. This was why Max had preferred living at Northfield Hall: there, everyone accepted a new order, and he did not constantly have to battle with himself about what was natural versus what was right.

Returning to Montchampion Manor had returned him to the world he had grown up in. The one that had taught him that nobility had more privileges for a *reason*, that servants were servants and laborers were laborers and the unlucky were unlucky all to keep society functioning the way it must.

Sometimes, it seemed so much easier to go back to believing in that order than to wake up each morning and fight tooth and nail to change it.

When it encroached upon Ellen's happiness, however—or, for that matter, the life his children would grow up with—Max had no time for it. "You are correct that Ellen is not prepared to be a countess like you. I love you, Mother, and I respect that you behaved as you considered right. You must now respect that Ellen—and I—do not intend to behave the same way. There *is* change coming to Montchampion Manor, and while you may think it is all Ellen's doing, it is actually mine and hers together."

Seeing his mother open her mouth to interrupt, he held up a hand to stay her reaction.

"Now, I shall require as little of you as possible. You may still have your tea and your silks and all the other luxuries to which you are accustomed. In return, you must stop trying to mold Ellen in your image. She is Lady Meretta now, not you."

"You invite chaos into our home." There was fire in her eyes but ice in her words. "You will end up murdered in the streets like my poor papa and mama."

"The problem then was that the poor did not have enough. We aim to change that here precisely so that our family is not overthrown by violence."

But his mother was no longer listening. She rose and pulled the velvet rope in the corner of the room to summon a maid.

Their afternoon tea was over.

"It is right of you to protect your wife," she said, gazing out the window, "but you are going about it all wrong."

"On that, I am afraid, we shall have to disagree."

The Storehouse

Ellen did not accompany Max and Mr. Nixon to review the rest of the park. She did not have it in her heart to hear Mr. Nixon list the reasons why they needed to repair the Grecian folly instead of tearing it down—nor could she stand to see Max pacify the man once again.

She did, however, steal Max away the next day for a tour of the storehouse.

This had been one of her first initiatives upon arriving at Montchampion Manor. Traditionally, the Hainsworth family kept all the harvest from its home farm, the meat from its butcheries, the butter and cheese from its dairies, and so forth for its own purposes. If there were any surplus, they sold it on market day. On holidays—or if a tenant was so badly in need that they would absolutely starve if no one intervened—Lady Odette might deign to visit the rows of leased farms to distribute wicker baskets full of foodstuffs that would last for about a week.

Ellen set that to rights. Now, anything that was not immediately consumed was brought to the storehouse. Everyone who lived on the premises of the park had permission to come fetch whatever they needed, whenever they were in need. Even the great house's kitchen staff had to stock their pantry from the storehouse's supply.

Formerly a faux hermit's cottage, the building had been rebuilt under Ellen's direction to become the storehouse. Its stone walls had been reinforced, and Ellen had built the shelves inside it herself. She arranged for maids to clean it twice a week and, in a concession to Mrs. Smith's fear of thieves and vandals, hired old Green from the village to lock and unlock the door. In the first month of Max's absence, she had spent her evenings carving a sign that now hung over its entrance, with a quote from Sir Francis Bacon:

Hope is a good breakfast, but it is a bad supper.

Just nearing its clearing on the cart path through the woods refilled Ellen with optimism—look what she could get done, if she were only allowed to!

She brought Max in the gig, as he complained he had spent too much time in a saddle for the past week. He draped his arm behind her, legs spread forward as far as the gig well would allow, looking no longer like an earl but instead like the arrogant, confident man she had fallen in love with.

Things had been better between them for the last day. Better, but not yet back to before.

Ellen was trying very hard to believe that Max had been faithful—to both their marriage and their ideals.

"How was your morning with Mr. Nixon?" she asked once they were out of earshot of the great house.

"Deadening. I know I must give a damn about drainage, but to hear about it for a whole hour..." Max slid a smirk her way. "To tell you the truth, my mind kept wandering back to you. Imagining what we might get up to this afternoon."

His hand curled around her ribcage just beneath her shoulder, tugging her towards him for a kiss.

Ellen permitted him to peck her cheek, then elbowed him back into place. "This afternoon you are seeing the progress I have made around here. I'm sure that is the excitement you refer to."

"Surely." But he straightened and said more sincerely, "I am of course eager to see what you have accomplished. Nixon said I wouldn't recognize the hermitage at all."

"Certainly he meant that as a compliment." Her sarcasm was borne of experience: every step of the way, both Mr. Nixon and Mrs. Smith had tried to obstruct her storehouse project. Mr. Nixon kept telling her it would disrupt the economy of the estate (which he failed to grasp was one of Ellen's objectives), while Mrs. Smith was afraid the whole thing would be plundered within a fortnight.

Max replied, "He is, like most people, afraid of what he doesn't understand."

Ellen didn't care to feel empathy for Mr. Nixon, who had plenty of resources to his name except for kindness. She focused on turning the horses onto the wooded path that would lead to the storehouse.

Max touched her back once more, only this time it wasn't flirtatious. "You don't really mean to harp on old Nixon, do you?"

"I wouldn't call it 'harping.' I am bringing to your attention his multiple failings, and I will continue to do so until the situation is remedied."

Max received this in silence. He reached out his opposite arm and touched the tree trunks as they passed. "I thought you wouldn't feel so strongly about it after the other afternoon."

A chipmunk darted out ahead of them on the road. Luckily, the horses were calm; they had traveled this path a hundred times, and no small rodent could spook them.

Meanwhile, Ellen racked her memory to understand what Max meant. "What happened the other afternoon?"

His palm tightened against the fat of her back. "What do you mean, 'What happened the other afternoon'? It was one of the most unforgettable afternoons of my life!"

She understood from that vigor, and the flush of his skin, that he was referring to their argument and intercourse and all of that.

She simply didn't know what it had to do with Mr. Nixon.

"Why would relations—as unforgettable and wonderful as they were—why would they lessen my dissatisfaction with Mr. Nixon?"

Max leaned back again, having lost some of his bluster. "Well, wasn't most of your dissatisfaction with me?" Fumbling, he added, "I mean to say, you were very unhappy with me, yet you were unable to express it to me directly. I thought perhaps you were using Mr. Nixon as an outlet for that, and now that we have resolved the issue, that you would see the situation with Mr. Nixon a little more clearly."

"I am a well-bred, educated, competent woman, Max. I am more than capable of being dissatisfied with both you and Mr. Nixon at the same time for completely different reasons."

She reminded herself to pause. Her heart was racing; she pressed her lips together and waited until it no longer felt as if it would leap from her throat. Then, more calmly, she replied:

"What I see *more clearly* is that you do not understand the situation at all. Mr. Nixon is not some kind old gentleman whose self-respect you are preserving. He is a willful obstructor. He hears what I plan to do and goes out of his way to make it difficult to achieve. He disrespects me, and therefore he disrespects you, and yet you refuse to so much as redress him."

Max cut in, "—and *so*, you are dissatisfied with *me*."

"Yes, because of how you respond to my dissatisfaction with Mr. Nixon!" Ellen had to loosen her hold on the reins or else hurt the poor horses. "Among other reasons."

"I do not disagree with you that he merits a reproach. Even a sacking. I am biding time, that's all. When playing chess, one must not respond to the other player's actions but instead continue with one's own plan."

"Oh, I cannot abide another chess metaphor!" All men *did* was compare their lives to chess games, as if life really could be reduced to sixty-four squares of black and white pieces. As if there was ever an *end* to the struggle in life.

As if a queen really did have more power than a king.

It made Ellen want to chase down every imported ivory chess piece and throw them all in a great bonfire.

"Carpentry, then," Max said, his tone growing steelier. "You mustn't stain a piece of wood immediately. You must first carve it, then sand it. Consider this the sanding phase. Montchampion Manor is not yet ready for its final stain."

She didn't like that he thought he could win her over with a little sweet talk about carpentry. Nor did she like to compare their plan to a *stain*. In poetry, that was too often associated with shame.

No doubt Mr. Nixon did think their plans would stain Montchampion Manor. No doubt that was why he thought himself righteous for disobeying her every request.

"You must also be careful not to wait too long," she replied to Max, "or else the rain might come and rot your wood away."

Max touched her shoulder. "I will not wait too long."

She knew he meant it as a solemn promise. But in her view, he already had. They were losing this year's harvest to Mr. Nixon's wheat; they were still purchasing small amounts of tea and sugar and tobacco to appease Lady Odette; they hadn't even begun to discuss a new name for the estate because Max worried it would cause too much consternation to everyone already living there.

The longer they allowed the status quo to remain, the harder it would be to change.

But they could not resolve the argument now. For they had arrived at the storehouse, and old Green had already emerged to open the door to them.

Max climbed down from the gig feeling the worse for wear. He didn't know how he and Ellen had ended up arguing. He had been trying to keep things light. He had, in fact, pictured them flirting their way to the storehouse, declaring it a success, and stealing away to their rooms again for another blissful afternoon during which he could prove to his wife exactly how much he loved her.

Instead, he followed Ellen into the storehouse with a knot in his stomach.

When he had left for London, the storehouse had been in the midst of its transformation. He paused to admire the new wood sign above its door. There were signs like this one all over Northfield Hall, and just seeing it, with Ellen's perfectly carved letters, made him feel at once more at home and as if he had been transported to some strange land.

Inside was different, too. In Max's childhood, the hut had been a simple folly, with nothing but some aging chairs and a pile of firewood inside in case a guest got caught wandering the park in the rain and needed a place of refuge. He was quite certain it had been a favorite spot for illicit trysts.

Now, the walls were neatly lined with shelves, and more rows of shelves stood free across its length. A second room had been built as a cold pantry. Everything was neatly labeled—in Ellen's handwriting, he couldn't help noticing—and organized according to category: grains, pickled fruits and vegetables, dried herbs, smoked meats.

Its order was so perfect that it was almost beautiful.

"Have you been keeping up with the log?" Ellen asked Green, who had been blathering about how grateful he was for the job. She stood by the entryway, where a thick record book of creamy paper waited to track how much of any supply was removed from the storehouse.

Green tugged on his ear. "I've been doing it just as you showed me, my lady. I look for the picture of the cheese or sausage or pickled radishes or what have you, and I draw a mark beside it."

Ellen peered at the book. "Is this for today alone?"

"No, ma'am, that is for the whole month."

Max chose not to go look over Ellen's shoulder. He was not here to manage the storehouse; he was here to celebrate one small success at Montchampion Manor with her.

Still, he noticed her frown. "Hardly anything has been removed..." Unsaid was the second half of her sentence: *if the logbook is to be believed.* Green was an old man, after all, and it would be easy for him to nap by the fire instead of monitoring the supplies or properly filling out the logbook.

He might even be one of those folks who didn't want the estate to change at all.

Max watched Ellen smile at Green despite all of these possibilities. Giving the man the benefit of the doubt, one of Max's favorite qualities about her. "Hasn't anyone been coming to take what they need?"

"Well, Ginny and Penny—the kitchen maids, ma'am?—they come most every day. Bertrice at the lodge house, too."

"What about tenant families? Or the groundsmen? Has no one except house servants come?"

The man tugged at his ear again. "I'm sorry to say no, ma'am."

The knot in Max's stomach grew tighter. This was supposed to be something Ellen could hold onto. The success she could remind herself of while they bided their time to change the rest of the estate.

Max reviewed the shelves again, which now looked awkwardly full. The food was all stored to last, and yet what would happen to the sacks of flour if they sat in the storehouse all winter?

Ellen, too, had turned to the shelves. Carefully, she said, "That is a shame."

"If I may, ma'am, there are folks who could use this food, more than the storehouse does anyhow. The Buckle family—they live in Farmer Row—their two boys caught a bad fever and have been laid up for days." Max received a nervous look from Green, as if the man were waiting for permission to say something more. Max attempted not to glare. Green said: "The dowager countess, ma'am, would have been visiting with a basket, so as to make sure they don't do without."

Max should have followed his better instincts and quelled the man with a glare. The whole point of the storehouse was to eliminate the need for a family to wait for bad luck to receive largesse from the estate.

"They need not go without," he corrected Green. "They need only come here and take what they want. If none in the family are able, they could send their neighbor or a friend or even a messenger to Mr. Nixon that they require delivery."

Green, white with apprehension now, replied, "Yes, my lord, only they could do with a basket, on account of the fever."

As much as Max knew that nothing about the situation was Green's fault, he wanted to pummel the man. What was so difficult about understanding that anyone could come take supplies at any time?

Ellen stepped to Max's side and placed a hand on his forearm. Their eyes connected, and he saw in hers a calm patience that belonged to Northfield Hall.

Then Ellen turned back to Green. "You are absolutely correct, Mr. Green. I shall go this afternoon. Would you help me select the supplies for them?"

It was another tool of hers, a magical way to earn a person's approval. Green lit up and started ticking off a list: sausage, cheese, flour, eggs, pickled vegetables, and potted meats. Ellen would have thought of them all on her own, of course. She started marking down on the logbook what she intended to take, and Max served as footman to cart the items from the shelves to the back of the gig.

For those small moments, he felt like Ellen's trusted partner again.

When the gig was groaning from the weight of all the food, Ellen declared they had enough. "Thank you, dear Green, for your help. I shall visit you again soon!"

Green fumbled out some sort of reply. The obsequiousness he had greeted them with had dissolved into something smaller and more sincere.

At least they had that as a victory. Max lifted Ellen onto the gig and climbed in, seizing the reins before she could. "May I take you to the Buckles, my lady?"

But, out of sight of Green, she didn't smile. She only closed her eyes and said, weighted down by exhaustion, "Yes, thank you."

The knot in Max's stomach returned.

They hosted the rector and his family for supper that night, which meant as soon as Ellen and Max returned from taking supplies to the Buckles, she had to close herself up with Slater to change into appropriate evening attire. Slater insisted on fixing Ellen's hair in a fancy concoction of braids and curls and a silver chain. "I won't have

Lady Odette saying you look like a governess," she said when Ellen objected. "I aim to build a reputation for myself as a proper lady's maid."

"Why, so you can desert me?" When it had come time to leave Northfield Hall, Ellen's maid Leyla had chosen to remain, so Ellen had hired Slater through an agency in London. At nineteen, Slater had only ever before been a chambermaid, but Ellen liked to give people a chance to prove themselves.

Especially young people like Slater, who had a vision for herself that included happiness and prosperity.

Still, Ellen wasn't prepared to let Slater go any time soon. Sometimes, it felt like Slater was the only one in the whole household who didn't want to see Ellen pack up her bags and return to Northfield Hall.

"Of course not. I only don't want any of the whispers about you to be about *me*." Slater said this guilelessly, her words formed around a grip of hairpins between her teeth.

It was not news to Ellen that people gossiped about her. The London papers loved to report on her family, which was one of the many reasons she hated going to town.

Even at Northfield Hall, everyone had seemed to know her news without her saying. Each one of her pregnancies had been common knowledge almost as soon as Ellen herself knew; with Robert, the whole of Northfield Hall had found out before Ellen even had a chance to write Max in London with the good tidings.

The whispers at Montchampion Manor, however, were not happy exclamations. They were, apparently, repetitions of Lady Odette's latest setdown. Repetitions no doubt embellished with some nasty words.

When the former butler, Robson, had given notice in a furious tantrum, he had said, "I cannot work a single day more for the devil's harpy."

Ellen had held her head high and given the man his full year's salary anyhow. She had not cried in front of him, nor even in front of Slater.

She knew Robson wasn't the last to call her that, though. And each time she thought about it, her heart clenched and her stomach heaved and she wondered how on earth she could last another second in so terrible a house.

There was no wondering, however, only doing, and so once Slater finished her hair, Ellen went down to the correct sitting room and hosted a perfectly fine meal with Reverend Dean, his wife, and their three adult children. Lady Odette made only one underhanded comment when she asked Mrs. Dean, "Have you been to see poor Mrs. Buckle? Mrs. Smith tells me two of her children have caught a terrible fever. I would pay a call myself, of course, except I should hate to overstep."

Ellen forced an inhale before she responded with a reply that would be too unkind. She didn't get a chance to speak, however; Max cut in. "Lady Meretta and I looked in on the Buckles this afternoon, actually. The older boy is already recovering, and the younger one will hopefully take a turn for the better in the morning."

"I heard you brought them a lovely supply of food," Mrs. Dean added, with an admiring blush in Max's direction. "They are most grateful, my lord."

"It was Lady Meretta's generosity at work." He smiled at Ellen.

She didn't always appreciate Max's dining room charm. It came to him so easily that he could offer a smile here, a wink there, a mildly flirtatious remark across the table, all to make everyone in the room feel they were the center of the empire.

If she were being honest with herself, witnessing Max at the dining table always made her aware that her husband's charisma was not exclusively for her.

Tonight, however, she took his smile like a salve and smoothed it over her heart. It gave her enough fortitude to make it through supper, the drinks that followed, and seeing the Deans out to their carriage.

Still, it was not quite enough to keep the gloom from settling over her as she and Max retired for the night. He took her hand as they descended from the nursery to their suite, and he did not let go until they were in his sitting room. A fire blazed in the hearth; he had instructed someone to prepare it for their use, and that told Ellen he intended to have at least one of the many conversations they were due.

She wished they could go back to a life where they didn't have to have conversations. She wished their days were nothing but sunny mornings and stealing kisses while their children raced across grassy fields.

Wishes were no use to a countess, however, so she decided she had better get it over with. "I suppose you shall say the storehouse must be broken up."

"Broken up?" Max raised his eyebrows in surprise. "Do you mean put back to how it was before?"

Ellen looked into the fire, which leapt with gleeful abandon. "If the Buckles won't even come to take supplies when everyone knows they are in need, it isn't working the way it is intended. What else is there to do?"

Max leaned back in his armchair, hands linking across his stomach, still looking at her with that strange expression of surprise. "You would give up that easily?"

She didn't like the accusation couched in his phrase. "I should prefer to think of it as not letting the people who count on us starve."

"Correct me if I am wrong, but the storehouse is still standing this evening *and* the Buckles have enough food to host a feast."

"Only because we happened to visit the storehouse and Green let us know they were in need."

Max shrugged. "Does that make a material difference on the outcome?"

"Yes." He wanted to debate this as if they were in a gentlemen's club quibbling over the language of a bill, and Ellen only wanted to end her heartbreak for the day. "No one is using the storehouse. It is a failure. Something must be done, and I suppose the only thing to do is go back to how it has been done for the past twelve centuries."

"Not twelve centuries, I shouldn't think. Before Henry the Eighth did away with the monasteries, I'm quite sure they were the ones taking food to the poor instead of old Lady Meretta."

"Max." It was all she could do to get his name out. Tears stung her eyes and choked her throat.

And in an instant he was kneeling beside her. His palm landed on the nape of her neck, cupping her in that way that made her feel so safe and loved.

It almost worked.

"I'm sorry. I don't mean to make light of it, Ellen. You have done so much work on the storehouse. It is a thing of beauty, if I'm telling the truth. No wonder you are frustrated that no one seems to understand that."

She shut her eyes. She already knew what needed to be done; she didn't want him to try to break it to her gently. She only wanted it all to be over so she didn't have to think about it again.

"And you are right, as always. Things *have* been done in a certain way for a certain number of generations. Doesn't it follow that change won't happen overnight?"

"It has been months."

"It hasn't even been a full season." His thumb drew circles on the skin just below the back of her hairline. "My darling Ellen. When it comes to giving a convicted felon a second chance, you have endless patience. Can't you apply any of that to poor Montchampion

Manor, which has been wicked for so long that it needs a little more time to reform?"

Ellen wasn't sure what he meant. "Is this another thing we must wait to attempt next year, like getting rid of Mr. Nixon?"

"That would require us to do the setup work twice. No, I propose we keep the storehouse as it is. What we must do now is train everyone to use it properly. You are the visionary, so I'm quite sure you will come up with the proper solution, but perhaps it means asking Mrs. Dean to send messengers when she knows of someone in need who isn't taking their portion, or perhaps you must do more visiting until everyone understands its purpose. The storehouse isn't the problem. The people are. And you are such a miracle worker with people, I know you shall find a way to solve this."

She took a proper look at him. Kneeling beside her, hand on her neck, his eyes were so wide and earnest. There was no smirk, no little eyebrow quirk to suggest he was only humoring her, the way he did when she was expecting and demanded a jar of pickle juice followed by a spoonful of honey.

He might actually mean what he was saying. Ellen didn't want to risk getting it wrong. "You don't think I have failed?"

"No." Max scooped her into his arms now, half rising to meet her and half pulling her out of her chair so that his cheek could rest against hers. "You have not failed, Ellen. Ask me again in five years, or ten. Ask me again at the end of our lives. How could you fail, when we have only time ahead of us to make our changes?"

Now she lost control of her tears. Just a little. Just enough to release the terrible feeling that had been welling inside her since their argument on the way to the storehouse. They stung her cheeks, then fell to Max's neck.

"You will not fail," he promised her. "I have too much faith in you for you to fail."

Ellen wanted him with a fierce desire that felt both as old as her love for him and so new that she wasn't sure she had ever needed him so desperately. There was no word for what she did next other than seize: in an instant, his mouth, arms, hands, body were hers. They tumbled onto the floor, so close to the fire that Ellen could feel embers leaping at her skin. She ripped her fingers through his cravat and threw it to the floor. His dinner jacket went next, then his waistcoat, and then she pulled the billowing shirt from the waistband of his breeches and yanked it over his head.

She pushed him down into the nest of clothes so she could finish with his shoes and stockings and breeches. She didn't say anything, didn't want him to say anything, wanted only to have him inside her and ride him so that this feeling of lovely, desperate blindness remained with her as long as possible.

She kept her own clothes on completely as she straddled her husband's hard, bare cock. Max didn't object, though he did lever his hips so that she tipped toward him, and he raised himself on his elbows so he could kiss the wool bodice covering her breasts. Even through the thick fabric, she could feel the pressure of his teeth; it rocked her with a wave of promised pleasure. She wrapped one hand around his neck to keep him there and stabilized herself against the floor with the other.

They were off to the races. Max was so hard inside Ellen that she could feel him against every inch of her tunnel, and when she sat back at just the right angle, his tip jammed against its ceiling. It was intense, it was pleasure, it was too much, it was just right. She kept moving, kept jerking, kept riding, always trying to find the exact right feeling and then, when she did, loving it too much to stay there for long. She felt frantic and out of control and like a version of herself she hadn't known for years. Max had little to do, for Ellen wouldn't allow him anything: she held him in place with her quim and hips and spare hand. He was growing red faced, his own body quivering, and Ellen knew soon he would spend.

The doctors said he shouldn't spend inside of her.

But she wanted him to, so badly. She wanted to not have to worry about consequences. She wanted to make love to him with abandon, like they used to, and feel that it was right and good and exactly what she had been put on earth to do.

She wanted to be the only woman he ever fucked.

"Ellen." Max said it through gritted teeth, his eyes half shut from lids heavy with desire.

He was warning her. He was trusting her. Ellen was in control for the two of them right now, and she could either do what she knew Max wanted—remove herself before he spent—or listen to her desire and let him and the doctors be damned.

She wanted so badly to damn them.

Max panted, his whole face screwing into a question mark. He was moments away. Ellen could clamp her muscles around him and keep him inside and take the risk that his seed would kill her.

But Max didn't want her to. He had spent months not doing anything more than kissing her, not even asking her to suck his cock, all because he was afraid of them getting carried away.

She couldn't carry him away now. Not when she knew he was asking her not to.

Ellen allowed herself one last rock, so deep that she felt his balls slam against her arse. Then she rose off him.

Max gasped. His cock leapt of its own accord in the bare air, a white stream of seed arcing onto his stomach. His legs wobbled against each other as the impact of it all sailed through his body.

Ellen fell onto her back. Her quim quivered, demanding its partner inside it again. She felt every nerve there longing for something.

If she had stayed on top of him, she would have found it. She shut her eyes, trying to pretend that Max was still inside her, that she was still riding him, but her fingers felt too narrow, too cold, not at all right, and she dropped them in frustration.

Max's lips brushed against her ear. "Do you remember the first time we fucked?"

"In the rainstorm." Ellen would never forget it. He had claimed to be a rogue and yet, when she stripped bare in front of him, he'd wavered, asking permission instead of taking her the way she so obviously wanted to be taken.

It was one of the moments that had made her fall in love with him.

"I came first then, too," he murmured. She had forgotten that. She had been the one to remind him that time, for they weren't married and had no plans to be and she could not risk a baby.

It hadn't dampened her pleasure then. Why did it now?

"When I turned around, there you were, working yourself towards a peak."

Ellen did remember the next part: "Until you took over."

Max rolled to hover over her. Even with her eyes shut, she could feel his arms on either side of her hips, his knees by her ankles. Her skirts were already hiked up; he placed a light butterfly kiss on the inside of her knee. "Please, Lady Meretta, may I pleasure you tonight?"

Ellen opened her eyes to see her husband kneeling over her. Max was so handsome, too handsome to have ever taken notice of her. Too suave, too interested in the world beyond Britain, and he took too much enjoyment of London to be married to a country mouse like her. He should never have fallen in love with her. He should never have married her.

She did as he had earlier and rose onto her elbows, reaching a hand forward to run through his hair. "I don't want pleasure. I want to be yours and for you to be mine."

Max leaned his cheek against her hand. "And so we are. I am yours, Ellen. Only yours."

He hadn't had any business falling in love with her, but he had, and here he was, on the floor, ready to lick her quim for as long as it took for her to find oblivion.

Lying back, Ellen spread her legs, shut her eyes, and placed her hands over her breasts. "Fine, you may pleasure me. But you had better go get your new toy to do so. I want something big and hard inside me for as long as it takes."

"My darling, wicked wife." Max claimed a long, messy kiss. Then he leapt, naked, into his bedroom to fetch the phallus.

Ellen played with herself while she waited, and this time, she peaked after just a few practiced flicks of her wrist. She kept it to herself, though, and when Max returned, let him work on her for nearly an hour with his toy and fingers and tongue. In the end, she orgasmed more times than she could count.

Max could. As he lifted her into his arms and carried her to his bed, he said proudly, "Five times. I think that is our best record yet."

She kept the sixth to herself. "Tomorrow night, we shall strive to do better."

"One must always aim for progress," Max agreed. In bed, they snuggled against each other, legs and arms entangled so messily that Ellen couldn't tell where she ended and Max began.

Just the way she liked it.

"I love you, Ellen. Do you believe me?"

"Yes." It was the right thing to say. It was the right thing to do. And Ellen almost knew it to be true. So she affirmed it: "I do believe you."

The Rumor

The very next afternoon, Max decided to earn Ellen another ally at Montchampion Manor. He began with the obvious candidate: Mrs. Smith.

Max timed his visit to the housekeeper's office with the afternoon lull, when the household had finished with luncheon and still had an hour or so before it needed to think about supper. It was a quiet day, too, with no visitors. When he knocked on the door, he suspected he could hear soft snoring on the other side.

If she *had* been napping, Mrs. Smith was quick to recover. She neither blanched nor blushed when she opened the door to him; she dipped into a curtsy as if she had known he was coming. "My lord, how may I help you?"

"I was hoping to have a word. If you are not too busy at the moment, that is."

Mrs. Smith did not betray any surprise, even though she *should* have. It was irregular for the earl to speak to his housekeeper, and if he did need a word, it was expected he would send for her to report to him wherever he found convenient.

Perhaps Mrs. Smith really was unflappable. She had been hired into the household a decade ago, when Max was off gallivanting on the Continent. She was a short woman, not very old but neither very young, with fierce brown eyes and lips that never seemed to smile. Her dark hair was streaked with dramatic lines of silver. Max only had some idea of her personality because he knew the servants obeyed her word like law, the rector's wife always brought a paper-wrapped gift to Mrs. Smith when visiting, and Mother swore that hiring Mrs. Smith was the second-best decision she had ever made, the first being to bring her maid Petit with her from France.

All of that, and that Mrs. Smith obeyed Ellen's new rules as narrowly as possible. Case in point: as she stepped back to admit him into her office, he discovered a pot and half-drunk cup of tea.

"Lady Meretta only said not to serve tea to the household anymore," Mrs. Smith said when she saw him spot them. "She never said I had to stop drinking it." Her words were defensive, yet she delivered them with hardly any emotion.

This was an adversary whose emotions he could not easily play.

Max would use other tactics, then.

"While there is tea in supply at the manor, there is no sense in letting it go to waste. If you don't mind sharing, I shall join you for a cup."

Mrs. Smith hesitated a moment, weighing his words, then took a second cup from its rack and served him.

Max helped himself to the wooden chair in front of her desk and indicated she should sit in the old armchair by her hearth. The cups and furnishings were all castoffs from past incarnations of the manor house; Max recognized the upholstered chair from what had once been his grandmother's suite, and the china was white-and-blue scenes of Amsterdam that his father had brought home from a trip two or three decades ago.

Max made a show of taking a long sip of his tea. "Perfectly steeped. I never realize how much I miss tea until I have it again."

Mrs. Smith nodded.

"I shall tell you why I am here." A strategy he had learned from the great persuaders of Parliament: lull one's adversary into thinking one was being forthcoming, when in reality one did not reveal one's true motivations at all. "I am reacquainting myself with Montchampion Manor after my absence, and I should like to know how you feel the household is doing of late."

Fiddling with her cup, Mrs. Smith asked the floor, "How it is doing, my lord?"

"Lady Meretta and I are aware that we are, for all intents and purposes, newcomers to this great household. I rely on Mr. Nixon to advise me on the park, but when it comes to the house and the people inside of it, I consider you the authority. Now, I know when we first arrived and announced our intentions, more than a few of the household left. Has that challenged you? Have you found replacements to your satisfaction?"

"Have you been dissatisfied, sir?"

Max set aside his tea. He pretended he was Papa Preston with kindness in his eyes to try to put her at ease. "Not at all, Mrs. Smith. If anything, I must admit I am impressed. I know that more than one maid quit on the same day, yet the floors continue to be waxed and the windows shined and the meals served on time. You have managed the changes without permitting them to disrupt the household. I commend you."

She blinked at him. At last, a hint of color crept into her cheeks. "Thank you, sir."

"Has it been difficult to find good help to replace those who left?"

She looked down at her tea. She put it on the table beside her chair. She picked it back up. She put it down once more. Finally, she looked Max in the eye. "Begging your pardon, sir, but it is difficult to find folk who will work here. On account of all the things they hear. Rumors, mostly. Still, they believe them."

"What kind of rumors?"

Mrs. Smith said righteously, "I wouldn't dream of listening to them, sir. And if I hear anyone repeating them, I give them what for."

Max didn't believe her for a second. He played along anyway. "Still, you have a sense of what is being said, because it is making it hard for you to fill the positions."

Now she blushed, a deep scarlet that betrayed more emotion than any muscle twitching on her face. "It's indecent, sir. They say that…well, to sum it all up, if I may, they say that at Northfield Hall there are improper relationships, and that Lady Meretta should like to set up the same sort of improper relationships here."

It was vague. Almost too vague for Max to parse, though he guessed it had something to do with the rumors in London about Northfield Hall being so ridden with adultery and sodomy and other illicit acts that it was a constant orgy.

Mrs. Smith added: "The kind of improper relationships that make it hard for a mother to send her Martha to come work here, sir."

Max leaned back in his chair now to make it clear he was not upset. "How do you propose we put an end to that kind of talk?"

Mrs. Smith blinked. She reached for her cup and took a greedy gulp before replying. "Perhaps Lady Meretta could change her practice on imports, sir, to prove that Montchampion Manor is not turning into Northfield Hall."

Which brought them to the crux of the matter, the very reason why Max had called on his housekeeper on a rainy day: how could he get her to join their vision, rather than simply obey orders?

Max decided against pressing the issue just yet. He picked up his own tea again. "Tell me, Mrs. Smith. Are you from Norfolk?"

She leaned back in her chair once more. "Yes sir, from King's Lynn."

"And before you came to Montchampion Manor, did you work within the neighborhood?"

"I was in London for five years with a bishop's family. I didn't care for being beyond Norfolk. My sisters are still here, and all my nieces and nephews. I like to visit them when I can."

"There is no bond like that of family," Max said without meaning it. In his experience, family was more of a liability than a bond. Yet if it was what Mrs. Smith cared about, it was what he would adulate. "Nor is there a county like Norfolk. The beauty here cannot be found elsewhere."

"Well said, sir."

"When I first married Lady Meretta and lived at Northfield Hall, I was baffled by how everyone could find the green fields beautiful. They hadn't seen the marshes, nor the way the tide rushes in here. They don't know a thing about natural beauty."

The flat line of Mrs. Smith's lips lifted ever so slightly.

"I also thought I would spend all my days dreaming of coffee and sweet buns, since I could no longer have them. And cotton—oh, how I do love a fine cotton shirt."

"Linen does not wash the same," Mrs. Smith agreed.

"Do you know how cotton is produced?"

A little hesitation returned to Mrs. Smith's manner. "In the mills."

"Quite so. Well, first the cotton plant must grow, and it only does well in specific climates. The American South, India, Egypt. The fiber must be plucked individually from each plant, which requires very many people tending the fields. I speak of slaves, Mrs. Smith, who are given no chance to earn their liberty and are treated most cruelly."

She looked down, her lips murmuring a word of agreement that he did not hear.

"The fibers must be cleaned, and then they are sent to the mills to be processed into cloth. This is where so many English men, women, and children are employed. Then the fabric is dyed and printed and sold to the rest of us.

"Now, when I first visited Northfield Hall, I knew all of this, yet still I did not think there was any reason to throw out all my cottons. By the time I purchase it, the evil has already been done. If I were to stop placing my orders for new clothing or bedding or what have you, the plantations would still exist and the poor souls unlucky enough to be enslaved would still be mistreated.

"To be honest, I have gone along with Lord Preston's rules more because I agree with the principle of the thing than because I thought it would have an impact. In fact...you won't tell Lady Meretta this, will you?" Max hesitated, waiting for Mrs. Smith's nod of agreement. "When I inherited Montchampion Manor, we brought the practice along because I promised Lady Meretta I would, not because I had any particular faith in it."

The housekeeper didn't react, except that Max didn't think she was breathing. He hoped this was currying favor with her, as he intended.

If it got back to Ellen, he would have more apologizing to do.

"These past few months, however, I have been reviewing the accounts, and I discovered that Montchampion Manor orders two thousand pounds of cotton every year. That is across our clothing, upholstery, curtains, and other fabrics; it does not even include the cotton in other supplies like our candlewicks and ropes. We give the largest orders at three different mills, who in turn source from ten different plantations. One person giving up cotton might be a drop of water in the ocean, Mrs. Smith, but all of Montchampion Manor? We could help bring an end to the slave practice entirely."

With a great sigh, she put her teacup down. "You are telling me that if I want tea every day, I should look for employment elsewhere, sir?"

"That is one way to look at it." Max leaned forward. "Mrs. Smith, I should like to invite you to stay. Montchampion Manor *is* changing, but that does not mean it is deteriorating. Far from it. If you stay, you will help set an example for Norfolk—for all of Britain. You will prove how much power each one of us has to improve the world."

She didn't look particularly convinced. Max couldn't blame her; the same speech wouldn't have worked on *him* when he first arrived at Northfield Hall, either.

"Permit me to share one more thing I learned from Lord Preston." Max refilled her cup of tea as he said this, to her obvious shock. "When he first inherited Northfield Hall in the 1780s, the local parish supported almost ten percent of its people on poor relief. There wasn't much work to be had, and if a harvest failed, people starved. Ten years later, after Northfield Hall had begun splitting its profits among everyone who works there, that number was down to five percent. Now, forty years later, there isn't a single person relying on poor relief. Imagine, Mrs. Smith, if we could do the same for Norfolk."

The housekeeper was still inscrutable to him. She didn't drink the tea he had served her. "It isn't the natural order of things, my lord."

To which Max had only one reply: "How do you know?"

He did not wait for an answer. He knew better than to expect to change a person's mind with a single conversation. He had only wanted to help, to see if he could plant a seed in Mrs. Smith's mind that would grow against all the objections she held so strongly.

Max stood. "I shall not bother you any longer, Mrs. Smith. Thank you for sharing your tea with me. It is, I trust, our little secret."

With a wink, he took himself away from her office, shutting the door to give her privacy in his wake.

He hoped he had helped win Mrs. Smith over for Ellen.

Life settled around Max like the winter fogs that rolled in across the fields. He had always thought his father's country life boring and idle, made of nothing except rides across the park and afternoons drinking tea over ledger books. Now he knew it for what it was: one decision after another. Which field to drain, when to rethatch his tenants' roofs, how to advise the local parish on caring for the needy.

Unlike his father, however, Max made a point of not letting it take over every moment of every day. In the mornings, he breakfasted with Ellen and the children; when he had shorter rides across the park, he took Rosalind or Odette along; and he still reserved at least an hour a day to read the papers and keep abreast of parliamentary matters.

It helped that they did not do much socializing. Once or twice a week, perhaps, they hosted a neighbor for supper, and come Christmastime they would have a neighborhood party with multiple families staying over, but for the most part, Max could retire for the evening and have a few hours alone with Ellen.

He was busy and sometimes overwhelmed, but in all, he thought he might secretly prefer this life to his life at Northfield Hall. There, he had boasted no responsibility. All his energy had been devoted to his committees in the House of Commons, which, in the countryside, left several hours a day to fill. He had been happy to play with his children or read books on history and science.

Still, he was beginning to like being Earl of Meretta.

He was ruminating on this at the end of a long ride, during which he and Nixon had ridden out to the seaside to examine the family's holding of a small harbor. The wind was brutal at their backs, and a steady rain had begun to soak through both Max's hat and his oilskin coat, chilling him to the bone. He looked forward to getting home and changing into dry clothes, then sitting by the fire with the children to hear about their days.

He looked forward to Ellen curling up around him, a jumble of warm limbs, to return the heat to his extremities.

"I have hesitated to bring this up, sir, but I'm afraid I had better before we are too close to the house," Nixon said, bringing Max's attention back to the soggy present.

Something in Nixon's tone set Max on edge even as he asked, "What is it, then?"

"It is the rumors, sir." Nixon paused. Max resented that; it was as if Nixon wanted Max to ask for more information.

From Mrs. Smith, Max knew there were rumors making life difficult. He didn't want to know anything more about them. And so he didn't follow Nixon's lead. He remained silent, until at last the steward continued unprompted:

"Regarding Lady Meretta."

Again, the pause. As if they were in the pub and Nixon were throwing out just enough information to prove he would handle sensitive information with care. As if he expected Max to confide in him.

Max held his annoyance at bay. "I haven't the faintest idea of what you speak, nor do I want to."

"Ordinarily I would not elevate the subject, as you well know. Rumors are not to be listened to, much less repeated. However, I am afraid they are disrupting the harmony of the estate. Mrs. Smith cannot find the necessary maids, while only the worst kind of rogues are applying to work on the repair of our fencing."

"Because of a rumor?" Max tried to keep his tone light. After all, Nixon was surely exaggerating. Fence work did not require that many hands, in the first place, and it was more likely that Nixon wasn't offering enough pay to hire the right men than that anyone was turning work away because of a *rumor*.

"Because of what is being said about Lady Meretta."

Again, the emphasis on Ellen. Max's annoyance was beginning to morph into an old, dangerous anger. One that made him want to punch the lights out of anyone who so much as looked at Ellen or his children the wrong way.

He did not punch Nixon, but it was only through clenched teeth that he could reply, "You'll have to forgive me, Nixon, but no one has dared repeat it in my presence yet. What, exactly, are people saying about my countess?"

Nixon coughed. Max looked over to see him turning bright red in his saddle.

Served him right for listening to gossip.

"There are whispers that when she goes to the carpentry workshop, it is not to do joinery at all, but instead to…participate in nefarious activities."

"You'll have to be more specific. Do they think she is stocking up on weapons for a revolution? Counterfeiting money? Engaging in an import-export business?" All accusations that had been levied against the Preston family, with varying degrees of accuracy.

"The rumor is that she has taken the carpenters as her lovers, my lord."

An image rose, unbidden, of Ellen at the manor's carpentry shop, bent over the worktable, being taken from behind by the dark-haired man who worked there.

Max dismissed it—as well as the overwhelming spike of jealousy that accompanied it—as soon as it arrived. "Carpenters, plural? That is quite imaginative."

"They say it is how things are at Northfield Hall, and that she is trying to set up her harem here as well."

Fingers curled around his reins, Max focused on not overreacting to the words leaping from Nixon's lips. He pretended to find the whole thing humorous. "And how do they suppose I feel about the whole thing? Am I an ignorant cuckold, or do I go to her harem, too, and watch her enjoy her spoils?"

"Sir." This, apparently, was Nixon's breaking point.

Max was glad to have found it. The rumor was too ridiculous to be believed, which was why the steward should never have bothered with it in the first place. "Idle gossip is not my concern, Nixon. If we cannot hire people because they listen to it, then we will be rewarded by giving work to people with brains between their ears. Do not worry yourself over it, and do not repeat it to me again."

It did not occur to him to warn the man off repeating the rumor to anyone else.

Time healed all wounds, Ellen had heard, and so she kept trusting that with time, her life at Montchampion Manor wouldn't feel quite so wounded. Her family, at least, felt whole again with Max home: they even managed to all be together when Alexander took his first wobbly steps to get from Max's hands to Ellen's.

Her marriage, too, was beginning to feel more like it had before the news of Max's father's death. She and Max not only shared a bed again, but they tried to retire at the same time so that they could cuddle each other and whisper about the day before sleep. Max made sure to compliment her appearance every day, steal kisses when the servants weren't looking, and generally pay her such attention that she couldn't possibly wonder whether he loved her or not.

It all worked, until Ellen realized he was putting such effort into it. Then her whole world would shift for a moment, like the moon eclipsing the sun, and she would see Max as a philanderer trying to charm his way back into her life instead of a loving husband expressing the true depths of his heart.

Sometimes, she didn't know how to bring the sun back to see things clearly again.

Mostly, however, Ellen believed that Max was honest when he insisted he had been faithful to her. Had they been at Northfield

Hall, she would likely have been able to put all doubts behind her and continue with the life she so loved.

At Montchampion Manor, however, it wasn't so simple. Max tried to ease her way: he accompanied Ellen to the carpentry workshop and gave the head carpenter a stern lecture when the man tried to claim all their lumber had been stolen in the dead of night; he invited her to accompany them when he and Mr. Nixon had to survey this or that part of the park; he joined her in trying to learn and use the servants' names.

It still wasn't enough to convince the servants to trust her. While she forced herself to go to the carpentry workshop at least once a week—on the principle that if they got used to her, they would eventually welcome her—the carpenters continued to ignore her as if she were a ghost haunting their joinery tools.

And she certainly hadn't garnered any respect from Mr. Nixon, no matter how many times she posed an intelligent question about estate management.

It was too soon to measure their success, Max had told her, and Ellen was trying to believe it. When he and Mr. Nixon went on their all-day venture to check on the harbor, she mustered the fortitude to face the carpentry workshop again and devoted an afternoon to the gliders for a new rocking chair she planned to give Mrs. Buckle. The head carpenter glared at her upon arrival and she had to spend half an hour searching through the storeroom to find where they had hidden her tools, yet eventually she was able to settle in and lose herself to the wood.

Walking back to the manor house, however, she got soaked in the afternoon rain, and so she had to call for Slater to help her change before supper. The maid was quieter than usual, which made Ellen suspicious. On a typical day, Slater chatted easily about what she had heard downstairs or the challenges she had faced in finding the right mixtures to get a stain out of Ellen's dress or even just whatever news she had from her family.

Her silence now was enough to make Ellen uneasy. And as much as Ellen feared its cause had something to do with Montchampion Manor, she felt honor bound to ask after the maid's well-being. "Did something happen today to make you so unsettled this evening, Slater?"

"I'm not unsettled, ma'am," the maid replied as she dropped a box of hairpins to the floor.

"Distracted, then."

Ellen didn't mean it as a complaint, but the blood drained from Slater's face at this comment, and the girl stood up straight as a rod. "My apologies, ma'am, if I have disappointed you tonight."

"You have not disappointed me." Ellen turned in her chair so they weren't addressing each other through the warped glass of the mirror. "You are so quiet tonight, Slater, that I am worried about you. Are the other servants being kind to you?"

"Oh, ma'am." Emotion rushed into Slater's voice, and suddenly her eyes shone with tears. "It's not me they are being unkind to. It's you. Only I didn't know if I should say anything. Gossip isn't worth repeating, my mother always told me, and no one with the common sense they were born with should even be listening to this rumor."

It took hardly any coaxing from there for Slater to tell Ellen the whole bloated story: that Ellen forced the carpenters into sexual acts each time she visited the workshop; that at Northfield Hall she had kept a different lover for every day of the week; that none of her children were fathered by Max. Slater had heard a dozen versions already, and she had first caught on to the whispers just the day before.

"Did one of the new people start the stories?" Ellen asked, surprising herself with how calm she sounded. Her voice was steady, as if she thought this was as amusing as Rosalind believing that honey was made from the crushed honeysuckle petals, when in reality, her heart dropped heavily in her chest.

Papa always laughed at the cartoons the London newspapers printed about the family. Sophia was known to cut them out, sign her name to them, and send them back to the illustrator.

Ellen had never found it amusing to know strangers were saying terrible things about her.

It was worse to hear that her own household was making them up.

"I don't know, ma'am. I heard Lady Odette's maid Petit whispering about it with Nurse Kathleen a few days ago, and I told them to mind their own business, but then I heard two of the maids talking about it while they were washing the floors today. When I told *them* to keep their thoughts to themselves, they told me it was a known fact and they had every right to discuss it with each other on account of not being sure if they want to remain employed in...and I beg your pardon, ma'am, but this is the word they used...in a 'harem.'" Slater's face darkened with a blush. She was looking everywhere except directly at Ellen.

"It is *not* a fact." Ellen swallowed to keep the nasty fear swirling in her stomach from overwhelming her. "I have never...that is...none of it is true, Slater. When I go to the carpentry workshop, I work with wood. I do carpentry. That is all. I have never been unfaithful to Lord Meretta."

The denial skipped like an echo across her heart.

It sounded like Max, insisting that he had never been unfaithful to her. Insisting that she had listened to a rumor, albeit one whispered by his own mother, and that there wasn't any truth to it.

But Max's taking a mistress in London would be fulfilling his destiny as a titled peer of the realm.

It wasn't anywhere as outlandish as a countess keeping a harem of carpenters as her sexual servants.

"I know it, my lady." Slater surprised Ellen by holding her hands, as if they were bosom friends.

And, apparently, she *was* Ellen's only friend at Montchampion Manor.

"I have said so to everyone who will listen. I told those maids they must have been dropped on their heads as babies if they could believe such a thing and that if I heard them so much as thinking it again, I would report them to Mrs. Smith for improper behavior. I only wish

I could say as much to the whole household. And...well, I heard the grooms making jokes about it, too."

Which meant the whole estate was afire with the rumor. Ellen doubted all four dozen people who worked for the family believed it, but it was an exciting story—and no one here needed any prodding to think the worst of her.

With a flash of nausea, she wondered if Max had heard it.

She squeezed Slater's hand. "Thank you for telling me, Slater. It is good that I know. Now it is not your concern. I shall handle it from here."

How she would handle it, Ellen wasn't sure. Most likely, she would have to give up the carpentry workshop. She might also need to discuss the matter with Mrs. Smith to penalize anyone repeating the rumor—a punitive approach that went against the grain of Ellen's soul. She preferred to lead by bestowing everyone with her good faith and waiting to see how they would rise to the occasion.

The problem at Montchampion Manor was that no one was willing to offer her the same faith in return.

For the time being, Ellen would hold her head high and pretend the rumors simply didn't exist.

The strategy worked through dressing in her best dinner gown and descending the main staircase towards the blue drawing room. Before she could even turn down the corridor, however, Mr. Nixon intercepted her, his head crooked in his most obnoxious faux-obsequious manner. "Lady Meretta, if I may beg for just one moment of your time."

Ellen wasn't sure she was up for a conversation with Mr. Nixon. Whatever he wanted to discuss, it would be something that upset her: a masked scold for showing too much interest in the estate or a pronouncement that the flax seed had all been destroyed and they couldn't possibly plant anything but wheat next year.

She assented to speaking with him, however, and steeled herself as he ushered her into the music room. "I hope you found the harbor in good condition."

"Absolutely, ma'am, nothing for you to concern yourself with."

She refused to bristle. Ellen knew enough about the *ton* to know that many ladies took an interest in running their estates; Mr. Nixon objected not because she was a countess but because she was a Preston. Well, she would not give in to his game.

"I'm afraid I must speak to you about a most sensitive subject. An indecorous subject, in fact." Mr. Nixon tucked his chin, pantomiming a caring steward.

Ellen knew before he said it that he was about to confront her with Slater's rumor.

"There are some unspeakable things being said by the household, ma'am."

The man was actually going to try to tell her people thought she was fucking carpenters on her spare afternoons. It was one thing for Slater, her maid, to inform her in the confines of her bedroom, where women could whisper about things without embarrassment.

Ellen couldn't breathe at the thought of Mr. Nixon trying to discuss so inappropriate a subject with her. She drew her shoulders into perfect posture as she managed to say, "Then it is best not to repeat them."

"Unfortunately, I'm afraid that something must be done. The rumor is rampant and is causing good workers to turn away from the family."

Ellen wondered what his plan was. Would he hint at the rumor but never say it? Would he hold its vague specter above her head to force her to bring tea back to the estate?

Would he threaten to tell Max?

Whatever Mr. Nixon planned to do, Ellen decided she would force his hand. With her most countess-perfect diction, she prompted him: "What is the rumor, exactly, Mr. Nixon?"

She expected him to blush. She thought he would stammer or retreat or otherwise realize he had taken the whole thing too far.

Instead, Mr. Nixon didn't so much as blink in consternation. Ellen realized belatedly she was not baiting him but rather the reverse.

He *wanted* to tell her about it.

He had orchestrated this whole conversation so that his lips could form around the words: "That you are a whore, Lady Meretta."

She should have slapped him. She should have dismissed him on the spot. She should have done anything rather than, frozen in horror, ask, "And what do you propose I do?"

"I'm afraid the only solution I can think of is for you to quit Montchampion Manor and return to Northfield Hall indefinitely."

The Point of No Return

Ellen couldn't hear her own thoughts for the frenzy erupting inside of her. Her instinct was to accept Mr. Nixon's suggestion politely, flee the room, and fume for the rest of the night.

But this was a bridge too far. He had called her a *whore*, and now he dared suggest she leave.

This was no misguided servant trying his best to protect the family. Mr. Nixon was mounting a personal attack against Ellen—and she knew she needed to listen not to her instinct but to the anger whirling like a tornado of fire inside her body.

"How dare you, sir." She summoned every vertebra of her spine to its tallest height. She glared at him as if her eyes alone could reduce him to ash. "You forget your place."

The irony, of course, was that Ellen had never cared about rank. Most days, she wished everyone else could forget that she was the countess or, before that, the baron's daughter. She wanted nothing more than for everyone to be on equal footing.

But Mr. Nixon preferred reality, and so Ellen would take pleasure in reminding him exactly who in the room had been born with the right pedigree.

"My place is to consider the best interests of the park, ma'am, and it has been clear since the day you arrived that you have only the worst interests of the park in mind."

"It is not for you to disagree with me—"

Mr. Nixon interrupted her. "I wouldn't mention the rumor to Lord Meretta, if I were you. He told me he has heard of it and that it has confirmed his suspicions that neither Master Robert nor Master Alexander are his true heirs. It would be better for you to take your leave tonight and send word after you have returned to Northfield Hall."

And the man actually dared to step forward, as if to shepherd her like a dog from the room.

"How dare you, Mr. Nixon!" Ellen cried as his fingers reached for her elbow. "Unhand me, and see yourself from the property at once. You are dismissed."

He snarled, some nasty word about to leap from his mouth—when Lady Odette swanned into the room.

"My dear Lady Meretta, I just heard you speaking in the most unladylike tones. Whatever is the matter?"

Ellen's hands were beginning to shake. She turned them into fists to keep anyone from noticing. "Mr. Nixon has said the most offensive things to me. I have dismissed him from his post."

"Oh dear." Lady Odette pursed her lips and looked at Mr. Nixon, as if Ellen had reported that he'd stepped on her toes at a dance. "Surely you did not mean to offend Lady Meretta, dear Mr. Nixon?"

Suddenly, the man was obsequious, dropping into a graceful bow. "Lady Odette, how kind you are to give me the benefit of the doubt. Indeed, it is a dreadful misunderstanding, nothing more. I had wished to advise Lady Meretta that there are offensive rumors making it difficult to keep the household in order."

"Ah. Yes, those rumors. A very delicate situation." Lady Odette smiled at Ellen now, tilting her head so that the candlelight sparkled off her diamond earrings. "There, you see, *ma chère*? You cannot blame the messenger, even if the news is unhappy."

"I can and I do. Mr. Nixon, in case you did not hear me, you are dismissed. Leave immediately."

"Oh, but you cannot do that," Lady Odette objected, and she even rushed to Mr. Nixon's side and draped a hand over his shoulder. "Mr. Nixon is a devoted servant to Meretta. You cannot dismiss him on a whim."

The man gloated at Ellen—an open, toothy smile that made her stomach turn.

"Mrs. Smith!" Lady Odette cried out. The housekeeper, who had been passing, stepped into the music room, every step as slow as if she were approaching the guillotine.

"Yes, my lady?"

"Ask Lord Meretta to join us. We have a most unfortunate misunderstanding to settle."

Ellen felt the whole house slipping out from under her, as if she were falling backward and there was neither floor nor ground nor even Arabian carpet to catch her.

There was only an abyss, one from which she could never retrieve herself.

"We do not need Lord Meretta to settle anything," she insisted. "I have instructed Mr. Nixon to leave."

But Mrs. Smith was already on her way through the labyrinthine house. Mr. Nixon said to Lady Odette, "I am in your debt, ma'am. It is to your credit that you can see my good intentions at the heart of this matter. I am only thinking of the family and how best to protect it in these difficult times."

Nodding, Lady Odette admonished Ellen, "This is why one must be discreet, my dear. One may do anything so long as there is no talk of it, but gossip is the ruin of many a lady."

To which Ellen could find no reply. Denial hardly even crossed her mind; she was trapped in this upside-down world in which the mother of her husband believed petty, incredible rumors instead of trusting Ellen. She wanted to cry out in anger. She wanted to pound her fists on the floor and demand that Lady Odette try seeing things from Ellen's perspective for once.

She wanted to go home to Northfield Hall and never return to this hell.

Max arrived quickly. Mrs. Smith stepped into the room behind him and shut the door. Ellen knew it was to protect them from being overheard by anyone else passing through the corridor, but the click of the latch in the doorjamb sounded terribly like the locking of a prison cell.

Lady Odette spoke before Ellen had a chance. "Meretta, you must clear this up. Your dear wife is upset and has taken it out on poor Mr. Nixon. She is trying to dismiss him from his post. I explained to her that only you can do that, but we need to hear it from you."

Her French accent was almost completely gone as she enunciated her way through the speech.

Max looked at Ellen. He, too, was dressed for supper, except his lacy cuffs were tied up by ribbons to his forearms, his fingers stained with ink. His expression was unreadable, even to her, though she had studied him for all nine years of their marriage.

"Mr. Nixon was most offensive to me, and so I dismissed him." Ellen did not want to repeat what the man had said. She did not want to *have* to repeat it. She had been telling Max that Mr. Nixon was trouble; she had been begging him to get rid of the man; and this was what it had come to.

If Max had any amount of faith in her, he wouldn't require any further details.

"I did not mean to be offensive, my lord." Mr. Nixon pitched each word to clearly imply that her hysterical female sensibilities were the source of the whole trouble. "Lady Meretta misunderstood my intentions."

Ellen still stood as tall as she could; her hands were still fists at her side; her anger still funneled out as a glare. She focused it on Mr. Nixon again. She did not dare look at Max as she waited for his response.

If his chess game required Mr. Nixon's presence at Montchampion Manor, then she would admit defeat. She would retreat to Northfield Hall with the children, and she would leave the whole of Norfolk to Max and his family.

It was up to Max, and she would not watch as he made his decision.

Max stepped forward to stand between her and Mr. Nixon. It was not a smile; it was not a hand on hers or his arm around her waist.

It felt almost the same, though. Especially when he turned to the steward and said, "The countess has dismissed you, Mr. Nixon. Why are you still here?"

Max was not a man like his father, who believed that everyone except marquesses, dukes, and the king would dance at his orders. Still, he was accustomed to the people at Montchampion Manor heeding his word; on the rare occasions when he had dismissed a person from their post, he had never before had them stick around to plead their case.

He was not sure how to handle Nixon, who remained in place beside Mother. The man didn't even look alarmed. In precisely the same tone he had used when Max was a boy caught in a caper, he said, "Don't be a fool, sir. This is a misunderstanding. I said nothing to offend her ladyship."

Max threw his shoulders back, as if that would prove he was, in fact, the earl and not a child running around playing at it. "She has dismissed you, Mr. Nixon. That is enough for me."

"And so you would turn out a loyal family retainer on nothing but her word alone?" Nixon put on a pathetic face. "What will become of me if you turn me out? I'll have no place to live, no reference to my name, sir. Mrs. Nixon and I shall be beggared. All because your lady holds a grudge against me when I have done nothing except serve your family? Your father would never stand for this, sir, and neither should you."

"You have done plenty," Max replied. "You have misinterpreted her instructions or canceled them outright at every chance you got, even when I have told you to make her wish your command. My father would not stand for insubordination, and neither shall I."

Nixon looked around the room. Mother still held onto him, as if by touching the steward, she could keep the status quo of Montchampion Manor intact. By the door, Mrs. Smith watched silently, her expression inscrutable as ever.

Max imagined Ellen behind him as strong and unwavering as the Tower of London.

"Permit me to explain myself," Nixon said, his voice breaking a little with nerves. "I did not mean to cause offense. I was trying to impress upon Lady Meretta the severity of the rumors being circulated."

Now fury surged through Max. "I told you not to mention that vile gossip again."

"To you, sir, and so I thought I had better discuss it with Lady Meretta. Something must be done, or else Mrs. Smith will never be able to keep the household together." Nixon gestured to the housekeeper. She raised her chin, but neither assented nor dissented. "I repeated what has been said to me, nothing more. I did not mean for Lady Meretta to take it personally."

Max could pummel the man for even thinking about the rumor in Ellen's presence. "You disobeyed me, and you disrespected the countess. If it were anyone else, Nixon, I have no doubt you would advise me to dismiss them immediately. As you have been dismissed."

Nixon fell to his knees. He bowed his head. He stretched out his arms like a squire serving his knight. "I did not mean for you to take offense, Lady Meretta. I meant only to advise you on a solution that might protect you as much as it protects the family."

"Have a heart," Mother said, holding out a hand to stay Max. "Dear Mr. Nixon has been here longer than you have been alive. He did only what he thought was best. Forgive him. Give him a second chance to prove himself."

"Please. I am sincere," Nixon pleaded. "I see now where I erred. If you were to show me mercy, sir...if you were to bestow your faith upon me, I would be in your debt. I will do as you wish, even if Lady Meretta bids me to dismiss my own sons from their posts. I did not mean to let you down, my lord. Please, allow me to prove myself to you now."

If it were not such an urgent moment, Max would withdraw with Ellen to discuss the best course of action. But this was an instance when Max needed to be decisive. He needed to make it clear to Mrs. Smith and Mother and all of Montchampion Manor exactly how he meant to go on.

If only he knew what Ellen wanted him to do.

His father would never have tolerated such offensive behavior—not even from Nixon—and would already have called in the footmen to escort the man from the premises. But Ellen didn't want Max to be like his father. *Max* didn't want to be like his father. He wanted to be fair, kind, and controlled by reason instead of order.

Yet Ellen had wanted Nixon removed for months. It was because of Max that the man remained today; it was because of Max that the steward had been able to repeat a terrible rumor to her face.

So now, when the man insisted that he was being mistreated, when he begged for a second chance, did Ellen want Max to give the man their faith or turn him out? Dismissed without a reference, down and out on his luck, was Nixon not precisely the kind of candidate who would present himself at Northfield Hall and be welcomed with open arms?

Whatever he chose, Max knew he could not get it wrong. Not if he ever wanted Ellen to place her trust in him again.

He could not turn around and ask her. And so, without even a glance, he had to hold faith in his own good sense, and hope that she believed in him, too.

"Your repentance is too late, Nixon. Had you begged forgiveness after planting wheat instead of flax, we could have given it. Had you apologized when you realized you had offended Lady Meretta, we even then could have considered a second chance. As it is, I am afraid I do not believe you are in earnest, and so I must, for a final time, demand that you leave immediately."

Behind him, Ellen let out a breath.

Nixon straightened. His face twisted into a snarl. "Montchampion Manor won't survive this, mark my words. Without me here to keep watch, she'll hire highwaymen as groundsmen and you'll end up murdered in your beds."

Before Max's fingers could even finish curling into fists, Mrs. Smith stepped forward. As calm as if they were all discussing the marketing, she asked Ellen, "Shall I clear out Mr. Nixon's room, ma'am?"

And Ellen, with the same composure, replied, "Please. You may send his things by coach to the pub in the village."

Which meant Max had chosen right.

Relief made Max magnanimous. He didn't punch Nixon in the face. "You may take your horse. That way, you shall be off the property within the quarter hour. If I see you after that time, I shall have you arrested."

The man glowered, but at last, he seemed to comprehend he had to leave. He moved to the door.

He made one last threat: "This is not the end." Then, following Mrs. Smith, he departed from the room.

Crossing the room, Max flagged down a footman and instructed him to follow Nixon off the property. "If he does not leave, you'll lose your position, too."

"You are being too harsh," Mother said.

"I am not being harsh enough. If you disagree, Mother, you are free to establish your own household wherever you choose." Words Max should have said six months ago. He did not care that she glared at him, trying to force him to apologize. She had a generous living as dowager countess, and there were three houses within their holdings in which she could choose to live rent free.

This was not cruel. It was not even unloving. It was declaring himself to his mother and allowing her to respond.

At last, she gave up waiting for an apology. "As you say, Meretta." Lifting her chin so high that her tower of hair quaked, she swept from the room.

Finally alone with Ellen, Max allowed himself to turn to her. She looked every minute of her thirty-one years: worn, tired, and beautiful. But there was color in her cheeks and, when she met his gaze, Max fancied he saw the spark that had held the two of them together all these years.

When he held out his hand, she accepted it. That was the only invitation Max needed to pull her to his side and anchor her there with both arms wrapped around her waist. "I'm sorry."

"What for?"

"I should have sent him packing when you first told me about the wheat fields."

Ellen tucked her cheek against his. "You were giving him the benefit of the doubt."

"I wasn't listening to you."

"You listened. You thought you needed him more than I needed him to be gone."

"I need *you*." Max said it with his mouth buried in her hair. "I need you, Ellen, so much more than I need to be right about anything."

"You were trying to do what was right by Montchampion Manor. You have to think of the manor ahead of me. It is your duty."

"Hang the manor." He meant it. "Hang everything except you and the children. I would rather go back to Northfield Hall and install a steward here if it meant we could be happy. You are what matters to me. I should not have made you feel anything comes before you."

She kissed his ear, then his cheek, then his lips. Max had so many things he still wanted to say to her. Apologies, explanations, reassurances. He kissed her anyway with all the desperation in his body.

He had brought her to this hellish house. He had allowed a snake to remain in it. He had exposed her to a life where people whispered terrible things and her own steward threw rumors in her face.

He deserved her castigation, not this manna from heaven.

Ellen broke the kiss. Her lips were dark pink, her cheeks so red that they clashed with the orange of her hair. "I gather you have heard the rumor going around about me, then."

"I have. Wicked you. If you are keeping a harem of carpenters, you might at least invite me to join the fun."

Her smile was not nearly as carefree as he hoped it would be. "You know how I enjoy a tumble in the sawpit."

Max caught her chin in his fingertips and tilted it up so he could look directly into her gray eyes. "I didn't believe the rumor for a moment. You do not need to fear that, of all things. I know you too well to listen to such nonsense."

This time, she didn't even smile. She just looked at him with that earnest, questioning gaze that had always made him feel that he alone could keep her world spinning in the right direction. "What if I had set up with someone else? What if, while you were gone, I was so lonely that I took up with Philips the beekeeper?"

This time, the image of a dark-haired man taking her in an abandoned summery glade was not so easy to dismiss. Max remembered the beekeeper listening with excitement to Ellen's plan for the storehouse.

What if she had taken the man as a lover?

But Max couldn't believe it, not even for a second. Ellen was incapable of lying; if she had betrayed him, she would have confessed it long before this. "You didn't."

"But if I had?" she insisted. "Would you be able to forgive me? Or if you heard that rumor and believed it, would you be able to then forget about it, once I explained to you that it was completely false?"

Which was when Max understood what they were really talking about.

"I would have to find a way to forgive you. Even if I believed the rumor after you denied it, I would have to forgive you. I love you, Ellen, and I intend for our marriage to be a true one, and so there is no choice but forgiveness. Don't you think?"

"Yes." She pressed her palm flat against his chest, just below his heart. "I love you, too."

Which, he realized, they couldn't say to each other too much.

It wasn't that he didn't know it. It wasn't even that he didn't feel her love every day.

It was that there was still doubt between them about the other matter. So much doubt that the words themselves felt dangerous as Max said, "I wish you believed me when I say that I have been faithful to you."

"Most days I do." Ellen watched her hands on his chest. "I told myself I didn't believe it at all while you were gone. But then you came home, and it seemed impossible that you *hadn't* been unfaithful. That is what husbands do in London. Especially husbands whose wives are frigid and unhappy, which I have been."

"The same way that frigid and unhappy wives take up with beekeepers while their husbands are in London?"

"You are handsome and rich and titled. I know women flirt with you at every dinner party, and it would be easy for you, in a moment of weakness, to give in to their touch. You are a physical man. You need that sort of thing."

"Are you not a physical woman? I seem to remember you begging me for five orgasms in one night."

Ellen pushed away from him—not out of his arms, just enough so she could glare at him. "You are a flirt, a charmer, and a former rake who once dallied with the prime minister's mistress! Why *wouldn't* you find company while you were alone in London for four months? Why wouldn't you find someone prettier and more agreeable and who can be pleased with just some nice kisses and an expensive necklace?"

"Because I love you!" Max nearly shouted it, and he didn't regret it, even though the sound of his anger made Ellen flinch. "I love you, Ellen. I'm not an earl, nor a rake, nor even a husband. I am *your* husband. I was never tempted to break my marriage vows, but had I been, I wouldn't have done it, because I care what *you* expect from me, and I know you expect fidelity."

She stared at him, gray eyes wide, chest rising with a fast breath.

Max resisted the urge to fly away from her as he said, "Frankly, I am hurt that you would have so low an opinion of me. We have been married for nine years. Don't you know me well enough by now to trust me?"

Ellen reached up. Her hands cupped his cheeks.

He needed desperately to hear that she believed him. "I am guilty of failing you in many ways, Ellen, especially here at Montchampion Manor, but tell me you know that I did not betray you."

She kissed his lips—lightly, like a covenant. "I trust you, Max. I'm sorry I didn't have as much faith in you as you have in me. You've done nothing to deserve that."

He held her in place and took a deeper kiss, one that felt more true. "You believe me?"

She shut her eyes. Their argument remained as unshed tears beaded in her lashes. "The trouble is I have lost trust in myself. Everything I do here is wrong. The storehouse, the carpentry, even trying to learn the servants' names gets me into trouble. I don't believe my own instincts anymore. Even when they are right, like about believing in you."

The idea of Ellen doubting herself broke Max's heart. Ellen, who had always had such conviction. Ellen, who had shown him how to live by beliefs rather than cynicism. Ellen, whom he loved with every fiber of his being.

If she was faltering, he had no choice but to shore her up. "Your instincts are right. It's everyone else who is wrong."

"Mr. Nixon said I should go back to Northfield Hall. He said you could put the estate in order if only I left you alone."

The fact that she was repeating it meant that, even for a few seconds, Ellen had considered it.

She had considered leaving him.

"I should have punched him while I had the opportunity. You are my wife, Ellen. We knew we would end up here. I married you because I want you by my side here at Montchampion Manor, helping me make this a better place for everyone who lives here. I want you. I want your instincts. I want your vision."

Her eyes remained shut.

"What can I do to prove myself to you?"

At last, Ellen looked at him again. A smile—peaceful and painful at the same time—broke across her face. "Nothing. You have already proved yourself. I believe you, Max. I believe in everything you say." She gathered his fingers in her hands and said once more with emphasis: "I believe you."

"And you shall stay?"

Her smile eased. "You couldn't chase me away."

"Even if the carpenters call you a harpy tomorrow?"

"It takes more than a few insults to scare me off."

"What about my mother? What if she refuses to leave and always has something to say about your outfit?"

"I am far too strong willed to surrender to that kind of attack."

"What if the entire household starts whispering that I have taken up a lover in London next year?"

Ellen took his face solemnly between her hands. "You have my faith, Max. It shall not falter again."

"I shall not give you reason to doubt me." He stole another kiss. "I am beside you, Ellen."

"And I am beside you." She settled her old earnest gaze on him. "Montchampion Manor is ours. Together, we are putting it ahead of ourselves. We must. It is our privilege. We must not run away, no matter how difficult it is."

"In sickness and in health."

"Precisely." Laughing, Ellen kissed him again. Then she swung out of his arms. "Now, my appetite has vanished. Care to take me upstairs to see if we can locate it?"

The Unveiling

From her spot at the top of the front steps, Ellen could hear every footstep that clipped across the marble front hall. First came the children, in unsteady pitter-patters and runs, with the slow plod of Nurse Kathleen behind them. Then there was Lady Odette in slippers so delicate that her weight whispered across the floor. Last was Mrs. Smith with perfectly even footsteps, followed by a marching army of maids and footmen.

Ellen turned in time to see the whole group joining her on the front step. The children were excited; Lady Odette looked as if she were attending a funeral; Mrs. Smith managed not to betray any emotion at all.

Ellen felt a stirring of something in her stomach. All morning, she had been unemotional about this. It was only a little ceremony, something to mark the start of their new era. It hadn't even been *her* idea; she thought it was a little trite and might invite sneers from the servants and laborers, but Max insisted it was important to announce the occasion.

Now, seeing everyone gather behind her—and below, in the drive, watching the stable boys and grooms and gardeners and everyone who could take the walk to the manor house congregate—Ellen began to think this might be a good idea after all.

It was nice to see everyone in one place. Promising, too, that they carried neither pitchforks nor tar. Mrs. Buckle even smiled and waved at Ellen.

Perhaps this really was an opportunity to reset relations with everyone.

"Where is Meretta?" Lady Odette asked, suspicion lifting her voice. Ellen could hear what she was suggesting: that at the last minute, Max had abandoned the idea, had abandoned Ellen, and would be found somewhere embarrassing, like in the barn with the dairymaid.

"He is coming presently," Ellen replied confidently. He *was* a little late, but that was hardly alarming. Earlier that morning, he had been in the village interviewing candidates for the steward position, and he needed to change out of his dusty clothes before coming down for the ceremony.

She touched the parcel beside her. It leaned against the wall, covered with an old flannel blanket that Rosalind had made prettier with embroidered flowers. She hoped they liked it. She hoped *enough* people would like it. Not everyone would; Lady Odette, for example, and her maid Petit would declare everything about it hideous. But Mrs. Smith—would she approve? Would Philips the beekeeper embrace it? And Mrs. Buckle and the other tenants?

Ellen hoped they would give it a chance.

At last, she heard Max crossing the marble entryway. He took it at a run, his boots slapping against the marble floor, only pausing as he came within view of the servants.

He was still buttoning his shirt cuffs.

"My apologies. I have not kept you waiting too long, I trust?" Max nodded at Mrs. Smith, kissed his mother on the cheek, and joined Ellen and the children.

"We have not given up on you yet." Ellen slipped her fingers in his just long enough for a squeeze. Then, for propriety's sake, she let him go. "Would you like to make a speech?"

If there was one thing Max enjoyed, it was a captive audience. Were Ellen forced to address everyone gathered, she would have kept it short, her voice trembling as it left her body. Max, however, lit up from within as soon as he started speaking.

He started by thanking everyone for gathering, then launched into a summary of the philosophy behind the practices of Northfield Hall.

"Some of you have known me since the day I was born. You know that for much of my life, I believed in the accepted order of our society. You may even know that I first went to Northfield Hall to prove how the model fails. *I* was the one proven wrong.

"You have heard rumors, but I know you are smart enough not to listen to that sort of talk. Northfield Hall is not about harboring violent criminals; it is about redeeming men and women who otherwise would be condemned to living by violence. It is not about encouraging licentiousness, but about making room for those who love each other to live an honest life. And, most importantly, it is not about stealing money from anyone. Instead, it is about sharing the wealth our land provides among all of us who live here.

"That is why Lady Meretta and I consider it our privilege and duty to bring the same model here. Your families have been so important to my family for centuries. Montchampion Manor has flourished because of the hard work you have provided us. Lady Meretta and I want us all to benefit from what the land earns us.

"You may be unsure whether to believe me. You may think that is all fine for Northfield Hall but you would prefer to keep things the way they are here. I ask you one thing: trust us. Give us your faith. Things will not be perfect as we make this change, but I promise you it will be worth it.

"Now, to celebrate this moment, Lady Meretta and I should like to make an announcement."

Max swept his arm towards Ellen, inviting her to join him. They had planned this part, and Rosalind, Amelia, and little Odette picked up the blanket, ready to whip it away for the big reveal.

"From now on, Montchampion Manor will be known by a new name. Beginning today, we invite you instead to call it Hope Hall."

He nodded at the children, and they pulled back the blanket to reveal the sign.

Ellen had spent the last few weeks working on it in her spare moments. It was large enough to hang on the front of the manor house, and she had painted it red with the engraved letters highlighted in white to make sure every visitor would notice it.

She held her breath, waiting to see how their crowd would react.

For a moment, they were met with silence. Then from behind her came a clap. Followed by another. Ellen turned around to see Mrs. Smith applauding, and all the house servants quickly following her lead.

From the crowd in the drive, Philips the beekeeper let out a whoop, which triggered a laugh, and soon the whole lot was noisily sounding their approval.

Max grinned. He slung his arm around Ellen's shoulders and in the other gathered the older children. "I told you they would like it," he whispered to Ellen.

How glad she was she had trusted in him.

She was trusting him in another venture, too: for the next few years, they were purchasing flax from nearby farms instead of replacing the wheat crop—but they would sell the wheat at cost, so that no one at Norfolk need worry about the price of grain. Ellen wished they could change more quickly, but she was choosing to believe that Max's vision for this compromise would work out.

She leaned into his warm, strong side. "I suppose there is nothing left to do but to hang it."

They had brought her tools and a ladder to do it right there, in front of everyone. Ellen intended to let Max do most of the work. Before he could even climb the ladder, however, it became a group project. Footmen held down the ladder, a groundskeeper climbed it, and Max handed up the sign for hanging.

As it was fastened into place, the crowd broke out in a song. It sounded like a hymn, one Ellen didn't know, and she could only smile instead of joining in.

It was nothing like Northfield Hall. It was Hope Hall, somewhere different, somewhere new.

Ellen was just allowing joy to wash over her when a cabriolet raced down the last curve of the drive. The driver pulled the horse to a stop so fast that the vehicle almost crashed into its backside. As it was, the whole gathering went silent and turned as one to take in the spectacle.

"Were you expecting a visitor?" Ellen asked Max, for the carriage and horse were finer than what the average Briton could afford.

"Not that I'm aware of. Were you?"

Ellen replied in the negative. Yet even as she did, the cabriolet door opened, and out spilled two people she knew very well:

Her sister, Caroline, and Edward Chow.

Even more alarming, they held hands as Caroline forged a path through the crowd and up the stairs to Ellen and Max.

"I'm terribly sorry to interrupt your..." Her eyes were wide, her skin pale, her chin raised high. "I don't know what Papa has written you about Eddie and me, but whatever it is, I beg you will give us the benefit of the doubt. We are in desperate need of your help."

Ellen looked at Max. Max looked at Ellen.

Together, they reached out to embrace Caroline.

Giving people the benefit of the doubt, after all, was their family motto.

Epilogue

1844

Twenty-Four Years Later

Getting from Dover to Hope Hall took longer than it should have. Max had arranged a coach and four to wait for her at the rail station, yet the luxurious private vehicle got stuck on a road overcome by sheep and then again in mud and one last time simply because the turnpike keeper couldn't be found to open the gates. By the time he was finally found in the local pub, it was nearly dark.

The coachman advised Ellen it would be dangerous to continue past the village to Hope Hall that night.

She agreed—it was far too likely a horse would put its foot wrong after sunset, especially since it was a moonless night.

But she had been traveling for three months. On the trip to and from Egypt, she had been forced to purchase goods imported from all over the world, eat foods she had never before heard of, and stay with strangers whose wealth she was quite sure was ill begotten. Worse, it was the longest she and Max had gone without seeing each other since their terrible year of 1820. Safety be damned: Ellen had no interest in remaining at the village inn—no matter how nicely they had done up a private bedroom for her—when Hope Hall was a mere seven miles away.

So she walked.

She didn't tell anyone because they would all try to prevent her or force some sort of companion upon her. As if a fifty-five-year-old woman were so frail that she would collapse from a bit of frigid air. As if she hadn't lived in this countryside for two decades. Ellen knew the paths as well as she knew the back of her hand. In fact, by walking, she could take some shortcuts through the flax and wheat fields that reduced the seven-mile trek to five and a half.

She made it to Hope Hall by midnight. It was clear the household was abed. A lantern hung in each room, in case a family member happened into it, but the servants were nowhere to be seen and the sound of the clocks chiming the hour echoed through the hall. Ellen took care as she walked down the gallery, through the ballroom, and past endless sitting rooms, until she reached the grand staircase. There, she peeked into the library—and saw the glow of a lit fire in Max's study.

Someone, at least, was still awake.

She made some noise as she approached so as not to alarm him. Yet when Ellen crossed the threshold into his study, she discovered that while Max was not in bed, neither was he awake.

He was bent over his desk, head cushioned in his arms, a gentle snore corresponding with the rise of breath in his chest.

Ellen grinned from the pure joy of seeing him again.

Perhaps she could have left him to sleep. But Ellen had just walked nearly six miles in the dark of night to see him again.

She took the final steps to round his desk, then draped herself over his back, her ear against his. She kissed his gray-stubbled cheek. "I'm back, my darling."

Young Max might have jerked awake, but this was old Max, nearly sixty, with a head full of silver hair and a body that creaked with every movement. First, his snoring stopped. Then, he murmured. Finally, he sat up. "Ellen?"

"I should hope no one else has been kissing you awake."

He stood so he could turn around. Beaming, he caught her in his arms. "Only my delightful grandchildren when they wake up before even their nurses." Pulling her close, Max kissed her on the mouth. Ellen had been yearning for it since the moment she had left. She wrapped her arms around his neck and pulled softly at his hair, soaking in the ecstasy of his touch. But Max ended the kiss before even letting his hands roam. "Davy came from the inn to say you were staying there tonight."

"Oh, is that why you decided to sleep with your work?" Ellen teased.

"I only closed my eyes for a moment."

"You were snoring as if you had been asleep for hours."

Max grinned sheepishly. "You have caught me. I am without reason when you are not around. You must stay with me always, or else I do not know when to eat or where to sleep."

Ellen lifted her lips to his again. Yet once more, after hardly more than a peck, Max reared back.

"How did you get here, then?"

"I walked."

"By yourself?" Reproach edged his voice.

"I didn't want to bother anyone else. I know all the shortcuts as well as Davy does."

Max frowned. "It is far too dark out for that. You could have hurt yourself."

"I took a lantern."

"You could have fainted and no one would have known to look for you."

Ellen squeezed his arms. "I am hardly that weak. I am a seasoned traveler now, you know."

"You could have been kidnapped by highwaymen."

"I wasn't."

He gave her the look he had always used on the children when they were being impossible. "It was a dangerous choice, Ellen."

"You are quite right." Now she slid her hands up to his neck again and dotted her nose against his. "What can I say? I couldn't think straight knowing you were so close."

At last, Max relaxed into her arms. "I am familiar with that affliction."

This time, when he kissed her, he didn't stop. They had been tearing each other's clothes off for thirty years already, and still, it felt as if the world might stop if Ellen didn't get Max's hands on her bare skin that very instant.

"You are the first living soul I have seen since leaving the inn," she murmured as her mouth moved to tease his earlobe. "No one else is awake."

"Even if they were, no one would dare enter my study without knocking," Max added.

"Then we are agreed."

Even as she said it, he lifted her by the arse and flipped her onto his desk. Papers crackled beneath her; neither of them paid any attention. Max's correspondence could be rewritten.

An unforgettable fuck on top of it couldn't wait.

After all, even though they had spent so many years almost perfecting the act, Ellen and Max must always aim for progress.

Author's Note

Ever since *The Viscount Without Virtue* ended, I have wondered how Ellen and Max would fare in their particular lifestyle. With Max off in London for much of the year, how did they keep their marriage strong? How long could I keep them happily at Northfield Hall? What would happen when Max eventually inherited Montchampion Manor?

Eventually, I decided to write their sequel. Usually, I turn to historical research to ground my stories. For *The Countess Without Conviction*, I ended up turning to the Orpheus and Eurydice myth. Some friends and I went to see the New York City Ballet's celebration of Balanchine, which included a performance of *Orpheus*. Sitting in the opulent Lincoln Center watching a centuries-old artform, I thought of how Max might see a similar ballet in his time in London, and I wondered how its themes would strike him. (Balanchine's choreography only dates from 1948, but the Orpheus-Eurydice myth featured in operas and ballets in the 19th century as well.)

From there, I used the questions about faith and trust from the myth to fuel the emotion of the novella.

There is some historical research that informs this story, though! I recently discovered Robert Owen and his communitarian followers. Born into the working class, Robert Owen was an industrialist who was very interested in solving the problem of poverty through community planning. In the first two decades of the 1800s, he focused on reforming his own mills, making changes such as restricting child labor, setting up schools, and establishing a sick fund. He and his followers then started setting up new communities founded on shared labor ideas, similar to our modern idea of a commune. Owen also advocated for easier access to divorce and equal rights between genders. It wasn't long before he was accused of being an agitator of the working class (by the government), of being a spy on behalf of the government (by the working class), and of being a corrupt influence who encouraged illicit behavior (by anyone who needed a moral high ground). I took some of the fear that accompanied his ideas as inspiration for what Ellen and Max might face at Montchampion Manor.

If you would like to read more about Robert Owen, I share my research on my website for my newsletter subscribers. Unlock that research by signing up for free:

bit.ly/katherinegrantresearch

As always, I am thankful to everyone who helped bring this book to fruition. Jen Trinh, my sister Sarah, and my husband all gave me early-reader feedback. Sara Israel at Thimble Editorial provided excellent and thorough copyedits. Julia Gerbach let me give her classical Orpheus-Eurydice paintings as cover concepts and created another gorgeous Prestons cover. Thank you also to my ballet friends Pam and Melissa for going to that fateful *Orpheus* performance with me!

Take a Tour of Northfield Hall!

T HE PRESTON FAMILY IS famous throughout England for their country seat, where they don't import-export goods, where anyone is welcome who needs a safe place to land, and where the laborers get a share of the estate's profits.

Keep exploring the world of Northfield Hall with an estate map and a 3-minute virtual tour of the great house!

THE PRESTONS NOVELLAS

Unlock the tour by subscribing to my newsletter:

https://bit.ly/northfieldhall

About the Author

Katherine Grant writes award-winning Regency Romance novels for the modern reader. Her writing has been recognized by Foreword INDIES Book of the Year Awards, the Next Generation Indie Book Awards, the National Indie Excellence Awards, the Romance Slam Jam Emma Awards, and the Shelf Unbound Indie Book Awards. If you love ballgowns, secret kisses, and social commentary, a book hangover is coming your way.

Katherine also hosts the Historical Romance Sampler podcast! Find out more at www.katherinegrantromance.com

Connect with Katherine on your favorite social media platforms:

instagram.com/katherine_grant_romance/

tiktok.com/@katherinegrantromance

facebook.com/katherinegrantromanceauthor

THE PRESTONS NOVELLAS

BB bookbub.com/authors/katherine-grant

g goodreads.com/author/show/19872840.Katherine_Grant

MORE FROM KATHERINE GRANT

Catch up on The Prestons series:

The Baron Without Blame – A Prequel Novella
He may not know her name, but that won't stop him from proposing a fake engagement...

The Viscount Without Virtue – Book 2
When she discovers her family's enemy is hiding in plain sight, what choice does a lady have but to seduce him?

The Governess Without Guilt – Book 3

THE PRESTONS NOVELLAS

One bored governess, one handsome doctor, and unchaperoned nighttime activities. What could possibly go wrong?

The Charmer Without a Cause – Book 4
Everyone knows that a happy marriage begins with a lot of money and one good lie...

The Sailor Without a Sweetheart – Book 5
Is love worth giving a second chance?

The Countess Without Conviction – Book 6/A Related Novella
Is Ellen and Max's marriage strong enough to weather this storm?

The Miss Without a Mister – Book 7
Two hearts, one vow, and a world built to keep them apart. Can true love conquer all, or is this romance destined for heartbreak?

The Widower Without a Will – Book 8
This secret love affair risks nothing except his legacy—and her heart.

Explore the world of Northfield Hall:

The Hellion of Drury Lane
Behind the scenes, drama cuts both ways.

It's In Her Kiss
No good deed goes unkissed...

Three Nights With Her Husband
On this road trip, one bed is never enough...

Letters to Her Love
They are writing their love story one letter at a time...

In The Wide Open Light
She is willing to fight for reform, but will she fight for the man she loves?

Her Perfect Pirate
On this pirate ship, their fake marriage isn't meant to last...

Don't miss my first series, The Countess Chronicles:

The Ideal Countess – Book 1
Will a garden scandal lead to a duel at dawn, or happily ever after?

New Year's Masquerade – Book 1.5
With one night left of freedom, will Bernard choose to obey duty or follow his heart?

THE PRESTONS NOVELLAS

The Duchess Wager – Book 2
Will the duke lose the bet or his heart?

The Husband Plot – Book 3
What could go wrong when you marry a perfect stranger?

Thanks for reading!

I AM SO GRATEFUL you joined me on this journey back in time. If you enjoyed it, please consider leaving a rating or review on your book retailer, Goodreads, or wherever else you talk about books!

Until next time...

www.ingramcontent.com/pod-product-compliance
Lightning Source LLC
LaVergne TN
LVHW030318070526
838199LV00069B/6501